MEN OF SIEGE BOOK TWO

ZOOK

BEX DANE

All my love,
Bex Dane

Zook (Men of Siege Book Two) © 2019 by Bex Dane.

This book is a work of fiction. Any resemblance to actual events, persons, or locales is coincidental.

Published by Larken Romance 2019

Cover by Elizabeth Mackey Designs

Proofreading by The Book Wyvern[1]

Zook (Men of Siege Book Two)

"She sucked in my kisses like she'd been underwater without air for hours and my lips were an oxygen ventilator. Whatever she needed, my mouth provided."

Can the prisoner set the princess free?

Zook

My second chance at life is going better than I expected.

Got a job doing construction where my boss doesn't care about my criminal record.

A beautiful girl is teaching me to read and write.

Man, I'm falling hard for Cecelia. The Ivy League brunette with big brown eyes goes wild when I kiss her.

But she's hiding some kinda secret from me.

---

1. https://www.facebook.com/thebookwyvern/

She lets me in to the point I think we're soaring, then slams on the brakes.

She says her family has a hold on her that terrifies her.

She's letting fear win.

But I'm not afraid. Whoever I have to fight to make her mine, I'll do it.

Cecelia

If my life were different, I'd be Zook's girl.

I'd fly away with my sexy cowboy and never return.

But I'm a bird in a cage, owned by a royal dictator who will slaughter anyone I get close to.

We can only steal our intimate moments.

Because if we're caught, Zook's as good as dead.

Zook is a full-length standalone novel with a guaranteed happy ending.

"Suspenseful, heart-wrenching, smooth flowing, page-turning."

"Well written with great characters and hot steamy sexiness!"

Become a VIP

SIGN UP TO BEX DANE's VIP reader team and receive exclusive bonus content including;

- Free books

- Advanced Reader Copies

- Deleted scenes

- Behind-the-scenes secrets no one else knows

Send me bonus content[1]

---

1. https://www.subscribepage.com/bexzookdeletedscenes

Chapter 1

BOSTON, MASSACHUSETTS

Zook

"You might want to take off your hat, cowboy." The bouncer at the door of Siege nightclub handed me my Idaho identification card and took my last twenty bucks.

I adjusted my straw hat and gave him a tip of my head. "I'd just as soon keep it on. Thank you."

He opened the velvet rope blocking the entrance and let me pass.

Siege nightclub assaulted me as I stepped inside. Deafening music, flashing lights, wall-to-wall people, stuffy air. Not my scene at all. I just needed to find Tessa and then I could get the hell out of here.

All the men there looked like her husband, Rogan. Buzzed hair, obscene muscles bursting out of tight T-shirts. Swagger all over the place.

The camouflage splotches and brown nets on the walls made it feel more like these men were here to hunt, not unwind with a drink after work. The second-story balcony provided an ideal viewpoint to survey and pick off prey, and there seemed to be plenty of willing female victims on the dance floor.

Showing up here was dangerous. Tessa's husband hated me. But I'd spent the last twenty-one months in prison feeling bad about the pain I caused her, so I needed to talk to her tonight. Tell her I'm sorry. See if she'd forgive me.

None of the women looked like her. If she wasn't here, I'd wasted my first four days of freedom and spent all my money on a cross-country bus trip for nothing.

A pair of brunettes at the bar distracted me from my search for Tessa. One of them, the one wearing far less fabric, crossed her legs and flashed her thigh at two guys walking past. She was good-looking, and it might have worked if she hadn't jammed her straw up her nose instead of taking a seductive sip.

I chuckled as she banged her forehead on the bar. Poor girl. Taking it hard she totally blew her attempt to snag some attention. Her friend rubbed her back and talked in her ear. Must be nice to have your biggest problem be worrying about your lame-ass moves in a nightclub.

The music changed to some kind of rap song, and the girl perked up like a prairie dog. She tugged her friend to the dance floor and coaxed her to sway her hips.

Her friend stared up at the ceiling and drew my gaze to a girl suspended in a glass box. She looked dreamily at the box like she wished she could dance up there. Good to have goals, I suppose.

A jarhead approached them and blocked my view. I took the seat the girl had been sitting in and snagged one of the full drinks they'd left behind.

Some fruity shit, but after four days drinking nothing but bus-bathroom sink water, it was like Gatorade after a sweaty workout.

I wiped my beard with the back of my hand and resumed my search for Tessa.

The girl's friend, the one wearing the longer dress, broke out of the crowd and caught me drinking from her glass.

We locked eyes.

She glared at me like I was a criminal. Which I was, but still... it bothered me.

The navy-blue dress she wore seemed as out of place as these corduroy pants from back on the farm. She looked like a librarian in a jungle full of hunters. The women here had wild hair with jumbo curls. Her hair stayed where she'd carefully combed and pinned it back. A classy girl. And by the way she pegged me quickly as a bad guy, a smart girl. Staring at her made my gut stir like a worm digging into a stash of cornmeal. I didn't like the way she looked at me. I wanted her to see me as worthy.

Worthy of what?

Her acceptance.

Her touch.

Her heart.

A man worthy of her kiss...

Yeah, right. Like that would ever happen. She wouldn't lower her standards to be with a convicted felon who steals drinks in bars and can't write his own name. No. A girl like her could never be mine.

Chapter 2

HER HEAD PIVOTED AS she looked around for someone to save her from me. *Don't worry, princess. I won't hurt you.*

Her eyes blew wide one second before a strong hand hit my bicep and another gripped behind my neck.

My forearm twisted around the one gripping mine and I ducked, wrenching myself out of the hold.

I turned to find Rogan glaring at me.

What? You think I can't fight? You're wrong. Learned a few things in prison. First lesson is never let someone get you from behind.

Rogan lunged again and I blocked his right hook, but his left arm snaked behind my head and yanked me into a choke hold. My straw hat tumbled to the ground as he squeezed my neck between his barrel-like forearm and his elbow, hard enough to hurt, but not hard enough to cut off my air supply or break my neck.

Fighting the pain, I managed to land a series of punches to his ribs, but it was like hitting a steel wall. Right about now I could use Gustavo or Destry at my back, but I had no one. I rode alone tonight, and Rogan had me pinned.

Another man grabbed my free hand. Twisting it behind my back, they pushed me out of the bar and through a side door.

The chilly September air blasted my face as we emerged into a narrow alley, dark except for a few lights mounted on the brick wall. I stopped fighting for a second, letting them think I'd given up. They relaxed their grip on me, and I took advantage by kicking one guy in the ribs and elbowing Rogan in the face. That gave me the second of distraction I needed to break away again.

The other guy pulled a gun and aimed it at me. "That's enough."

I spit on the ground and swiveled my gaze back and forth between the gun and Rogan. We stood in a tense triangle, our chests heaving, the cold air turning our breaths to white smoke.

Rogan held his chin where my elbow nailed him. "Where'd you learn to fight like that?"

"Fuck you!" I eyed the gun still pointed at my chest.

The girl from inside came through the side door, my hat clutched in her shaking fingers. She stopped to pick up my hat? And followed a brawl out into the alley? Not smart.

Rogan squinted at me. "If you're here to talk to Tessa, you're shit outta luck. She ain't speaking to you."

"Get that fucking gun off me, Rogan."

"Hands up. We'll check you for weapons. Then I'll lower my firearm." The other man, the one with darker hair, spoke with a deep, no-bullshit tone.

I looked to the sky and raised my palms to the level of my shoulders. Rogan moved in and patted me down. He nodded at the man holding the gun who inserted it into a holster at his hip.

The tension in the alley dropped a notch as we all loosened our defensive stances. I exhaled a ragged breath into the cold night air.

"Rogan!" Tessa burst through the side door. Glittery cursive letters over her breasts bounced in the tight black Siege T-shirt she wore. Pink sparkly heels shuffled up to Rogan's side. Still pretty. Always was.

"Go away, Tess." Rogan didn't take his eyes off me.

"No. Is that Zook? Zook Guthrie?" Tessa's eyes grew round as she took me in. Apart from the disheveled clothes, the Zook she saw now was nothing like the Zook she knew. I spent every second in prison pushing my body to the max. Sit ups, push ups, running in place. Getting stronger and bigger. I was hard now. All softness gone. "Oh my gosh, Zook. What's going on?"

"Saw him messing with her drink." Rogan tipped his head toward the girl who looked like a librarian.

She took a tentative step forward and squeezed the hat so tight, I saw the top collapse. "He didn't mess with my drink."

Whoa. Didn't expect her to say that. Expected her to rat me out. Rogan wrapped his arm over Tessa's shoulder and glanced down at my hat in her hands. "You know him?"

"No. I don't. But I saw him. He moved the drink aside, but he didn't tamper with it."

This was technically true because I didn't mess with it, I drank it. Not sure why this girl felt she should lie for me though.

"Here's your, uh, hat." She shook the hat out, trying to get its shape back and held it up for me.

I reached out slowly to take it. She stared into my eyes, urging me to play along. Close up, she was even prettier than I first thought. Big brown eyes, glowing skin, a killer body. God, I'd give anything to have her go back inside and not watch this. What she'd seen already was humiliating. Now she was lying for me.

"Thanks." I ran my hand over my hair before popping the hat on.

"I'll ask one more time. What's your business here?" Rogan asked me.

"I'm looking for my parents," I admitted, looking at Tessa.

"They ain't here," Rogan replied.

"No shit? Aging religious freaks from Idaho don't hang at the Camo Club in Beantown?" Rogan grated on my last nerve. I wasn't gonna hurt her. Just talk to her.

"Watch your mouth, asshole, or I'll remove you myself," the man who had pulled the gun said. "I own this damn joint, and I'm not liking your attitude." He turned his attention to Rogan. "Fill me in. How do you know him?"

Rogan's gaze moved to the man who asked the question. "This is Zook Guthrie. Tessa knew him growing up in Idaho. He went to prison for assaulting her and another woman a few years back. Got a call he was being released, but I didn't expect him to show up here. I'm guessing he wants to reconnect with Tessa. That ain't happening." He turned to look at me. "She's my wife. You don't need to talk to her."

"He said he's looking for his parents, not me," Tessa said.

"And I said they ain't here."

Tessa put her palm flat on Rogan's chest. This seemed to calm him because his jaw relaxed, and the fire in his gaze dimmed. "I can help him."

"He's a fucking criminal."

Ouch, that hurt. It was true but hearing Rogan say it like that stung. Tessa and I had been close once. We were there for each other when no one else was. And even though it sucked to hear him talk about me like that, I was glad she had him. He clearly loved her and would protect her, which is exactly what she needed. She'd made life good for herself. I needed to do something similar with my life; I was just two years behind her.

"Tessa," I said and she turned to look at me. "I'm sorry. About what happened. I never shoulda let it get that far." Felt good to finally say it to her.

Her eyes softened like she'd found a lost puppy. Pity. For me. I hated that look all the time but even more when it came from Tessa. She knew me. We had the same story. She shouldn't pity me. "It's okay, Zook. You were caught up in my father's web just like all the others on the compound. You deserve a second chance. We all do."

That was nice of her to say, but, "I still shoulda put an end to it before you got hurt." This thought haunted me most nights in my cell, wishing I could tell her how much I regretted what went down.

Rogan nailed me with a dubious stare. If he wasn't here, I could talk to Tessa more, but we had an audience. I wanted to get her alone and tell her that if I had known the FBI was planning a takedown, I would've given them the info they needed earlier and she wouldn't have had to go undercover into the compound, putting herself at Jeb's mercy. Luckily, Rogan was there in the background and made sure she didn't get hurt.

"If y'all got this handled, I'm going to return to my office." The man who'd pulled the gun stepped back toward the door we'd come through.

"We're good. Thanks, Dallas."

The man he called Dallas stopped at the pretty girl who had followed us out. "You alright, ma'am?"

"Yes, I'm fine."

"Would you like me to escort you back into the club?"

"Actually, I'd like to stay here if that's alright."

Her voice was timid and shaky. Why would she want to stay out here in the cold? It was sorta like a train wreck. Maybe she couldn't look away.

Dallas nodded and returned to the club.

"I don't know where your parents are, Zook. But I can look for them for you," Tessa continued.

That was all I wanted. The reason I came all this way. To make contact, make amends, and make sure they're doing okay. "I'd appreciate that. My mom, if she's still in the Brotherhood, I wanna help her get out." From what I'd heard, people still followed Jeb from prison. He controlled the congregation from behind bars. I couldn't stand the idea of my mom suffering like she did before.

"I understand. Give me your contact info and I'll let you know."

Oh, hmm. Contact info. Shit. I shuffled my feet and glanced at the girl. "I'm in transition right now."

Tessa frowned and her voice grew concerned. "Do you have a place to stay?"

"Yes," I answered belligerently. The subway terminal counted as a place to stay.

"You know," Tessa continued, more casually, "Got a small school set up in Idaho for the boys from the compound."

Damn. Tessa always got on me about learning to read. "Don't start, Van." My voice came out tight. I did not want to talk about this here. In front of Rogan and the librarian. There were some things we shared she should keep private.

"I go by Tessa now," she shot back.

She'd always be Van to me. "I know. Still. Don't start."

"Don't start what?" Rogan asked.

My eyes passed over the girl again. She was listening with her ears perked at full attention. I muttered under my breath. "Fuck." Now she knew my greatest weakness. I needed schooling.

"Come by here tomorrow morning, Zook," Tessa pleaded. "I'll tutor you."

Oh man, Tessa offering to tutor me didn't sit right. Never did. She was damn persistent too. Always trying sneaky ways to teach me to read. She had even given me her journal and told me I had to learn to read to see what it said. I still hadn't read it, but I planned to. Soon.

Rogan's arm tightened around her shoulders. "No, babe. Not him."

"I'm not holding a grudge against him. He didn't hit me, and he was forced to do what he did. He's not a bad guy. He's good. He needs my help."

As she spoke I stared down at the ground. "I don't need no help. I just wanna find my parents."

"Why don't you call Destry? I saw him on—"

Oh hell no. My head came up and I shot her a warning glance. "I'm not speaking with Destry."

"That's a shame. You boys were so close."

A wince of pain passed through me. Tessa was scoring me deep with every word. Hearing Destry's voice in my head had become normal for me, and being apart from him, well, I missed it. Some pretty negative voices had taken his place. "Listen. I gotta go." I turned to the girl and tapped the brim of my hat. "Thank you for my hat. My apologies if your evening was ruined."

"No. I'm glad I could help clear this up." She had a gentle, smooth voice. Pretty and classy. Just like everything else about her.

I threw her a wink and a smile and she looked away. Shy. Cute.

"Come to Siege tomorrow morning, Zook." Tessa's repeated request drew my gaze from the girl.

I stared her down and gave her as much "drop it" in my eyes as I could manage. "Bye, Tessa." I turned and walked toward the exit of the parking lot.

Tessa called to my retreating back, a desperate edge in her tone. "Meet me here tomorrow, and I'll tell you if I find any info on your parents." The girl never gave up.

My hands made a snapping sound when they hit my sides. "Vanity manipulating me this time. Goddamn Barebones."

I didn't look back as I left the lot. Holy hell. That could not have gone worse.

Chapter 3

I MADE IT INTO THE Siege parking lot around eleven the next morning. My stomach growled and my feet weighed me down after only four hours sleep. But my curiosity and the persistent need to connect with someone who knew me drew me to the club.

Last night, I believed Tessa when she said she wanted to help. It felt good to have her eyes look kindly at me, like she'd forgiven me.

The girl I knew growing up wouldn't miss the opportunity to give me shit about learning to read. Even if her husband discouraged her, she'd do it. She'd be here today waiting for me. Least I could do was show up.

The empty lot told me the building was closed. No one answered my knock at the door. The concrete walkway surrounding the building looked clear. Tessa didn't come. Fine. Rogan might have won the battle. I was used to going it on my own. I'd just continue from here.

I turned to leave. To my right, where the walk turned the corner of the building, a flash of pink appeared and disappeared within seconds. What the hell?

"Someone there?"

I heard scuffling and the pink appeared again, a puffball rising from knee level to eye level. Even more pink emerged from around the corner.

A woman wearing a magenta coat and a goofy hat dusted herself off and bustled toward me. She raised her head and looked at me. Holy hell. The woman from last night. The stunning brunette I'd stolen a drink from.

"What the fuck are you doing here?"

"Um, hi, Zook." She tugged on the belt that was already cinched around her tiny waist.

Her eyes scanned my clothes. The only store open this morning was a hoity-toity men's shop, so I'd used the money I scored off the drug dealer I mugged last night to buy charcoal slacks, a collared shirt with buttons, and a midnight-black leather jacket shaped like a sports coat. The only thing I liked was the jacket. The long pockets hid the gun I snagged from the drug dealer. They didn't have any hats, so I was still wearing my straw hat with it.

She planted her feet in front of me and righted her shoulders. "I'm Cecelia." Her eyes brightened like her name should mean something to me.

"Nice. I dig that song, but I didn't ask your name. I asked what the fuck you're doin' here. Where's Tessa?"

The light in her eyes dimmed. "She sent me."

Tessa sent the girl who I'd stolen a drink from? The girl who watched the whole fight with Rogan last night? She overheard everything, and still she showed up here alone? Why?

"How long you been sittin' there waiting for me?"

"Since dawn." This girl had been sittin' in the cold outside an empty club all morning? Waiting for my ass to show up?

"Really. And do you have the information I need?"

"No."

"You know I'm an ex-con, right?"

"I know."

"Then what the fuck are you *doin'* here?"

She stepped back, finally getting the message she should be afraid of me. "Uh, well, I was hoping to tutor you."

I looked to the sky and laughed. I knew it. Goddamn, Vanity Barebones set me up. I made eye contact with Cecelia again. My laughter quickly cut off. "No."

Her head flinched back. I felt bad snapping at her, but all I wanted was to find my family. Not get sucked into some tutoring scam with some beauty queen in a pink jacket and a fru-fru hat.

"Now call Tessa and tell her to get down here and tell me where my parents are."

"I talked to her this morning. She hasn't found them yet."

"Great. Fucking great."

She smoothed back her hair, as if the pecan-colored locks had any chance of escaping the smooth mass of hair she had knotted at her nape. "It's only been a few hours. Give her some time."

This was true. Tessa probably knew this last night and planned to ambush me all along. "Fine. See ya, Cecelia." I tipped my hat to her and turned to leave the parking lot.

"Wait."

I ignored her and hummed the chorus to "Cecelia." Destry and I used to play that song on guitar.

Her boots tapped on the asphalt like she was running to catch up with me. When fingers grasped the crook of my arm, I spun on her. "What do you want?" Unless the answer was to fuck me, we were done.

"I want you."

Oh, now that was pretty close to *I want to fuck you*. Maybe I should give this girl a chance. She'd waited alone in a parking lot for me all morning. She *wanted* me. Plus, she was gorgeous and hiding a killer bod under that wool coat.

"You want me?"

"I mean I want to know more about you."

Too late. She'd already admitted she wanted to fuck me. And my sex-starved brain had already imagined yanking her perfect ponytail from her neck and pulling it like reins on a mare as she took my cock from behind.

Now normally I wouldn't use someone for sex, but I'd been locked up years with only a few sticky magazines and the occasional porn that made their way around the cell block. If she wanted to fuck, I'd entertain her tutoring ruse till I got her naked.

"Not here," I said.

"Where?"

A girl like her I couldn't take straight to a hotel. I'd have to charm the pants off her first.

"Lunch. I need food."

I was starving after spending all night walking, getting in a fight with a dealer, finding a hotel, then shopping for new clothes and taking the T back to Siege.

"I have a favorite bistro on campus." The hopeful glint returned to her eyes.

"What's a bistro? What campus?"

"Hale. And a café with the best macchiato you've ever tasted." She walked briskly out of the club parking lot.

I'd never tasted that and... "They don't let people like me on campus at Hale."

"Of course they do. Anyone can eat at the bistro."

We reached the entrance to the T. She took out her wallet, but I pushed it away.

"I'll pay."

"But..."

"I pay. No exceptions."

She relented and we boarded the subway train to Hale. We exited on a historic street with manicured lawns. Aristocrats and yuppies milled about the cobblestones. I might be wearing the right clothes today, but I definitely didn't belong here.

She approached a restaurant with a pink and white awning. I couldn't read the black letters scrawled across it, but wouldn't be surprised if it said "Fru Fru Bistro." I stepped ahead to hold the door open for her.

She strutted up to the counter and spoke quickly. "I'll have a prosciutto focaccia panini with gruyère and an espresso macchiato."

The cashier entered it in like he spoke the same secret language of socialites and uppity coeds at Hale.

"What would you like?" she asked me.

Fuck if I know. "Do they have food? And coffee? A boatload of coffee."

She stared at me blank-faced for a moment before turning to the cashier and smirking. "Make that two of the same."

He farted with his little tablet a bit more then looked up at her. "Fifty-three seventy-one."

Holy hairy balls. Fifty-four bucks? What the hell did she order? I paid the bill and pocketed the change.

As we sat at an empty table, I said, "Do those coffee beans come out of a golden goose's ass?"

She grinned and worked open the huge wooden buttons on her coat. "I don't know. When you taste it, you'll understand why students here pay top dollar for it."

Whoa. As she stripped her coat off, my eyes glued to the curves of her ribbed turtleneck sweater. It hugged her breasts tight, the bra outline visible. Bumpy like lace. Holy fuck, Cecelia was packin' heat. Totally worth fifty-four bucks and a T ride if it ended with those tatas in my hands.

"The days are cooling down fast." Her voice barely reached my ears.

"What?" Shit. Hmm. Her boobs totally distracted me. I forced my eyes to pupil level.

"It was so muggy here just a week ago. The cold is setting in."

Oh right. September. The change in seasons didn't matter too much in the slammer, and I knew shit about the weather in Boston. "Right."

"So, where're you from?"

"Federal prison in Colorado."

She took that in stride and didn't miss a beat. "Did you grow up in Colorado?"

"No." Her questions chipped away at my chances of getting laid. Telling her I was raised in a fundamentalist break-off sect of full-blown crackpots would not get me in there.

Luckily, the cashier arrived and delivered two plates containing triangular sandwiches with grill marks, melted cheese dripping over the sides, and two coffee cups small enough for Barbie.

I jammed a big hot bite of pan-whatever in my mouth. "Oh shit." I burned my tongue on the sandwich, dropped it, and gulped down some... fuck, hot as hell coffee. Shit. It all hurt and tasted good at the same time.

A giggle as delicate as windchimes made it through the chaos of my first bite of food.

With my tongue still tingling from the burn, and my mouth full, I said, "Shut up."

More windchime giggles followed. God, the sound of a woman's laughter. Something I'd always coveted but never had in my life. Not in any way I could call her mine. I risked another, much more careful, sip of the rich coffee, which tasted more like chocolate mousse. "Where the hell do I get one of those golden geese?"

Her giggles broke into unrestrained laughter, snorting included. She covered her mouth with her hand, trying to hide how hard she was laughing. Damn, that felt good. So good a man could spend his life bending over backward to hear the sound again. And other sounds. Mmm. What other wild noises could I draw out of Cecelia?

She chewed a nibble of sandwich. "So, Zook Guthrie. What are your hobbies?"

How did she know my name? Guess she picked it up last night. But still, she remembered it. "Do you know Rogan and Tessa?" I answered her question with a question.

"No. Just met them last night."

"You know my last name and I don't know yours." Let's see how she liked the third degree.

She looked down at her food and swallowed. "Boujani."

"Cecelia Boujani?"

"Yes."

Pretty and classy like her. "I build things." My second bite of the sandwich didn't burn my tongue and she was right. It tasted damn good.

"What?" She peered at me over her tiny coffee cup.

I swallowed down the bite I'd taken. In prison, it didn't matter if you talked with food in your mouth. At a bistro at Hale with a gorgeous girl, I needed to mind my manners. "To answer your question. About my hobbies. I build things."

"Like what kinds of things?"

"Mostly houses. I've been hammering and nailing since I was four. I can build anything. Specialize in woodwork, though."

"Wow. That's impressive."

And fuck me if she didn't sound honest. She sincerely thought I was impressive. Her eyes took me in adoringly. She wanted me. And the more we sat here, the quicker I wanted her to finish her food so I could take her to a hotel and make her come apart.

What kind of bra did a girl like her wear? My guess, pink lace. Sweet and shit. It would be so hot if my snobby librarian were hiding something freaky under there. Maybe some ruby satin or leather. Yeah, definitely a leather bra that barely covered her nipples.

While I was daydreaming, she'd removed a paper and pencil from her folder and set them square in front of me.

"What's this?" I leaned back and dropped my hands loose by my sides.

"Let's determine our starting point. Can you write the alphabet for me?"

I didn't pick up the pencil or even look at the paper. I just kept staring at her eyes. The color matched the chocolate coffee she'd ordered us with little flecks of cream mixed in.

My reflex reaction to this wanting-to-tutor-me shit was to shut the person down right away. Never let them get started or they'll push for more. But something in her eyes forced my mouth closed. Maybe it was the naive hope in her voice, or the nervous way she kept glancing down and then into my eyes again.

"Okay, then. Let me..." She made a few marks on the paper.

No, I couldn't push Cecelia away like the others who had come before her and failed. She was different. I didn't want to hurt her. And I really wanted to fuck her. Walking out now would definitely reduce my chances of ever getting that.

I placed my elbows on the table and leaned in. A faint fruity scent, like oranges, distracted me for a second. Of course, Cecelia smelled good. Everything about her was refined and delicious. "That's an *A*," I said, soft and quiet.

She grinned, proud of herself for getting a response out of me. "Yes. Good. You know *A*. So every letter makes a sound. The *A* says ah, like avocado."

Oh, now this was new. No one had ever brought food into the lesson before. "*A* don't say *A*?"

"*A* says *A* too. Sometimes. But it also says ahh, like in bad."

"A bad avocado." I exaggerated, wagging my finger like I was scolding said avocado. She watched my finger, and a giggle escaped her lips. Yes! I did that. I made the windchimes ring.

"Okay so... First we learn one sound for each letter, then all the variations and how it changes based on what letters are next to it." She drew another letter on her page. "The *B* says buh like baby."

Oh she was asking for it now. I had to sing it. "Like baby, baby, oh... Baby, baby, no."

Her eyes widened big and her brows shot up, then her entire face turned into a reluctant smile. Oh yeah, I had Cecelia as good as naked now.

I let her get through *C* and *D* with no jokes. The girl's cheeks were red enough. She glanced at me, expecting my joke. I held back and she shook her head and smiled. Okay. Tutoring could be fun with Cecelia.

"What's this one?" She drew more lines on her paper.

"*F*"

"No. This is an *E*."

Damn. "Right. *E*. Not wearing my glasses."

She squinted and scrunched her nose. Cute, but we'd reached a milestone. Cecelia now knew the extent of my knowledge didn't go past the letter *E*. She'd located my weakness. Now who was the naked one?

"Look at it like this." She drew a rectangle standing on its short side. "Imagine this box is the frame. Like a house. The letters all fit inside, but each in their way. Like custom beams. Curved, long, short. But they all need to touch the frame in some way to remain stable." She sketched an *E* inside the rectangle and traced it again. She drew another box, put an *F* inside it and said "*F*."

This made sense and I admired her for getting through to me when many girls had tried and failed. But... I wasn't here to learn my letters.

I sat back in my chair until I got her gaze to lift from the paper to lock with mine. "I been in prison two years."

"Oh. Um... I mean. I know."

The silence stretched out between us.

"Let's move forward." Her pen shook as she scratched out something. "What letter is this?" She looked up at me, waiting for my answer.

"You're missing my point. I been in prison two years. With all men. And you smell good."

Her mouth dropped open and she stared at me, frozen. "I do? Um."

"Your hair's shiny. Your voice is all feminine and sexy."

"Thank you," she said with a bewildered smile as more color rose in her cheeks. This was working. I had her stunned into submission.

I swiped my finger across her temple and around behind her ear. She closed her eyes as she felt my touch for the first time. Yes. I'm so in there. "Hard to concentrate on learning with you being all those things."

She blinked and her thick lashes lapped at the apples of her cheeks. "Well, uh, I understand that must be..."

I took her hand that wasn't holding a pen in mine. Her skin felt soft and gentle. Two things I had never had in my life. "Let's get out of here. I'm staying in a hotel."

Oh shit. That was the wrong thing to say. Cecelia shut down so fast, I could see the windows slamming and the closed sign coming up. Damn.

"I have to go." She scooped up her papers and threw them in her bag. "I'd really like to tutor you, but I can't uh, let it go any farther than that." She stood and clutched her backpack and jacket to her chest. Hiding from me.

"I'll be honest with you, CeCe." She stepped back when I used a nickname for her. "Can I call you CeCe?"

"Yes, uh. It's nice."

"Right. CeCe, I'm not really interested in you tutoring me. Although you're the hottest teacher I've ever had, and you've gotten farther with me than anyone else who's ever tried."

"I am? I did?"

I smiled. "Yeah."

She set her bag down on the table and dug through it. She pulled out a notebook and pen. "Take this." She withdrew a white sheet with lines and letters on it. "Let's meet again. We'll finish capital letters and start on lowercase." She shoved the sheet inside the notebook and tucked the pen in the spiral binding. She pushed the notebook toward me. "Trace the letters a few times. Keep looking at it. Try to memorize it."

I stood and shook my head. "I don't want you to teach me. I want something completely different from you."

"I'm sorry. I can't... I mean, I'm not interested in you that way."

Bullshit. This girl made no sense. She wanted me, she clearly felt the same pull I did.

"I don't believe you."

She bit her lip. "You don't?"

"I don't believe you don't want me too."

She looked around the bistro, her eyes on anything but me. Her voice came out tiny and pleading. "Zook. I'd be honored if you'd let me teach you."

"You'd be honored?"

"Yes. Just, please. Take the notebook. Bring it back to the library tomorrow at noon." She pointed out the glass door of the bistro. Beyond the massive lawn, there was a huge old building that looked more like a church than a library. "I'll be waiting. Bottom floor, center aisle."

She turned and ran out the door, leaving only the tempting scent of oranges behind her.

Well, shit.

Chapter 4

⸺

"THOSE GIRLS BEEN EYE fucking you." The man sitting next to me in the pub tilted his head toward a group of women across the bar from us. I'd wandered into an Irish pub for dinner a while earlier. Needed food after spending a full day roaming Boston and hitting up construction sites for work, only to be handed applications I couldn't fill out.

"Noticed that," I replied as I took another sip of my amber ale. My first fucking beer in two years went down sweet. I'd have to mug another dealer to buy my next one, but for now, this one was legit paid for, so I was taking my time enjoying it and listening to this guy talk.

We'd been shooting the shit for over an hour. What was his name again? Somethin' about bulls. Toro or some shit.

I hadn't told him jack about me, but when I asked where he was from, he started talking. Turns out he was an interesting guy. Retired Navy from Texas, ten years older than me, black hair, buff but not fat. Camo pants and a sleeve of tats under a black tee. Looked like one of Rogan's Army buddies.

We'd started talking horses and turns out he used to ride bulls for BRX. He had my respect then because I'd spent a fair amount of time around bulls and never had the balls to ride one.

"You gonna partake?" His question returned my attention to the girls across the bar.

A stacked redhead, a blonde with really long hair, not bad-lookin' girls. Fake as hell. I was aching to get some, but nothing about them was cute enough to motivate my ass out of this stool. Now, if Cecelia were sitting over there, I'd be all over it like a chimp on a jackknifed big rig spilling bananas on the freeway, but these girls... not worth the effort.

"Nah. I got a particular woman on my mind."

"Yeah? Who's that?"

"Her name's Cecelia."

He took another sip from his beer. He was on his second or third. "She on your mind or on your dick?"

"She's just on my mind right now. Working on getting her on my dick. You can have both those girls." The redhead giggled at her friend, thinking Toro and I were returning their attention.

"They aren't my type."

"What is your type?"

He stared at a spot on the wall. His voice grew deeper and he spoke in a darker tone. "The kind with no garbage attached. Like to take what I need and move on. Girls like that don't let you walk out after a fuck. They want to be held and shit, want to give you their number, start balling if you don't give them the baby treatment. I gave up on that a long time ago."

"I hear ya."

He set his drink on the bar and stood from his stool. "What was your name again?" he asked me. Maybe it was his fourth beer because he was a little unsteady on his feet.

"Zook Guthrie."

"Zook. Pleasure." He held out his hand for a shake. As I took it he said, "Torrez Lavonte."

That's right. Not Toro, Torrez.

"You Mexican?"

"Brazilian, Puerto Rican, and little French. Purebred mutt."

I liked Torrez. He was personable and humble.

"I'm a white-as-all-fuck cowboy from Idaho. Possibly a little inbred since my family was big on kissin' cousins."

He laughed at that but it was totally true.

"Well, I gotta be on the job site at the butt crack. So, I'll see ya."

"Jobsite? What kind?"

"Residential construction. Interviewing a new foreman. Lost my man last week. Got no time for this shit."

Ah, he was drinking his stress away tonight. I could help him with that.

I stood too and leaned in close to make sure he heard me. "I work residential. Custom builds, tracts, anything you need."

His shoulders pulled back, and he stared at me for a long time. "You lookin' for a job?"

"Just so happens, yes. I'm between builds right now." Like two years between, but he didn't need to know that.

He pointed at our empty bar stools. "Sit."

We returned to our seats and talked for three more hours. I told him I was an ex-con. He didn't seem bothered. Didn't ask details. He said he usually hired veterans, but he'd make an exception for me.

He offered me two grand a month, paid in cash. He asked me to act as foreman and live in the house while it was being built.

"I can do that." Very easily since I didn't have a place to stay right now and no money.

"You got sprawl?"

"You tell me what sprawl is, I'll tell you if I have it."

He chuckled. "Sprawl is the itch to work. Energy to act fast. You ain't got sprawl, you're a lazy slowcome-pokum."

"In my parts, we call that a pile."

He raised his eyebrows.

"Guess it's like a pile a shit."

He laughed. His eyes became serious and searched mine. "I need the details of our arrangement to be on the down low."

"Not a problem." I spent my life keeping secrets. Course I also used those secrets to bring a man down, but he didn't need to know that.

"Okay. I like you, Zook. You finish this build on time, I'll raise your salary and start you on five more homes just like this one."

"Oh, I'll finish it. You better hold up your end of the deal."

"I will."

"Where's the property?"

"Province Bluffs." I'd heard of the town where celebrities spend their summers. "New seaside estate home. Wall safes, escape routes, high fences, top of the line products and quality."

"Could build you a place like that with my eyes closed."

"Then it's a deal. You're my new construction foreman for the Province Bluffs build. We're working against a clock. You have until the beginning of June. I need someone I can count on to make this happen."

"I can do it. So, two thousand bucks a month for nine months?"

"Yes."

I shook my head slowly. "Not enough."

"You getting greedy on me?"

He'd made an incredible offer to a stranger, but I had to push it. "I have dreams. Big ones."

"Shoot."

"I'm gonna make a million dollars in the next year."

He whistled a high pitch that slowly decreased to a low hiss. "You set the goalpost high on your first season out of the locker room."

"I'm not dead. I survived prison with all my limbs. I fine-tuned my skills while I was in there. Now I'm gonna use them to my advantage."

"I like that, but in my business, a man has to prove himself before he can ask for favors. This first house is critical for you. No fuck ups, no overruns, no excuses. Get it done right and on time. Then we'll talk about profit share to earn your first mil."

"Alright."

"You come through for me, I'll put you in touch with my associates."

Wait. Stop. Red light. I knew this was too good to be true.

"What kind of associates?"

"The kind that take your back." Oh shit. I'd heard talk like that in prison.

"Listen, I appreciate that. But I'm a loner. Plan to be running my own operation within a year. Don't wanna get tangled up in any kind of family business." Hopefully that was general enough to cover any gangs, mafia, or syndicates he was involved with. If he had criminal ties, I wanted to steer clear of it.

"You'd make money faster if you had my kinda friends on your side."

Yeah, I knew those kinds of friends. So, I'd use Torrez to get started then move on before his friends sunk their claws into me.

"I've made a choice for my life. Nothin' illegal." Not anymore.

"I respect and understand. Wish I'd made that decision when I was faced with it." He nodded and stood again, this time more steady on his feet. "I'll make sure to keep you clear of that side of my business. You just manage this build for me."

"No problem."

"Good. I'll bring the architect's plans here in the morning, and we'll go over them. I'll take you to the site and get you started."

"Deal."

With our handshake, I had my first job in the outside world, a place to live, and a new boss with money to blow. Not bad for my first week out of the slammer.

Chapter 5

CECELIA

"No, Tessa. He didn't show today."

"Stay a little longer." She'd said the same thing every morning when she called to check and see if Zook came to meet me at the library.

"It's been two weeks and we haven't heard anything from him." I'd memorized every inch of stone and glass around the door as I waited here for the student who never came.

I shouldn't have offered to tutor him. I couldn't get too close with anyone while I was here in the States. Soraya and I had to follow the family rules. We were here to earn diplomas and nothing else. Once we finished, we'd return to Veranistaad and assume our duties as royal princesses. Duties that suffocated us and robbed us of all our dignity, duties that were forced upon us and beaten into us since we were fifteen. Duties we could not shirk because the consequences would be unbearable. Ivan regularly threatened to torture and kill us and anyone we cared for if he found out we had crossed the line with a man.

We shouldn't have even been at Siege the night I met Zook, Tessa, and Rogan. Soraya came up with these audacious ideas that we should date adventurous and brave men, soldiers or policemen with guns, so they would fight the family for us. She was even dating the guy she met on the dance floor, Cage. He was a Marine, but didn't seem like the kind of man that would risk his own life to save ours. I'd never ask that of someone who cared for me anyway.

"He's being stubborn," Tessa said. "His pride is holding him back, but he could—"

A man in a cowboy hat approached the door. "Oh my god!"

"What?"

"He's walking in!"

Zook sauntered into the library and paused to examine the three-story bookshelves on either side of the lobby. His face remained nonchalant, unaffected by the grandeur of one of the oldest libraries in the country.

"Gotta go." Setting my phone on the desk, I gulped down the sudden lump in my throat and stood to face Zook.

I gave myself the pep talk again. The one Soraya had been pressuring me to give up. *Just tutoring. Nothing else could happen. The risks were too high. Ivan would send Maksim after me, Soraya, and Zook. We'd all pay for my selfishness. I couldn't stand it if something happened to Zook.*

My heart melted when I saw the notebook he gripped in his left hand, dangling it casually at his side. He had saved it and brought it to the library. A small thing, but to me it meant I'd made the right decision at Siege by offering to tutor him. This could work out for him... For us... *No. Just tutoring.*

The slacks and dress shoes he wore the last time I saw him had been replaced with black jeans and pointy-toed leather boots. A new shorter leather jacket with a zipper covered his white button-down shirt. A midnight black suede cowboy hat hid his eyes from me.

More stubble dotted his angled jaw than last time and, in this setting, under these lights, next to the towering book stacks, he looked like a giant. A tall, strong, confident giant. He must be at least six-foot-five, maybe six-foot-six? The books he couldn't read didn't intimidate him.

In fact, the three-story stacks quivered in fear at Zook Guthrie's arrival in the Hale Library. That may also have been my hands shaking.

His lazy perusal of the books turned into a scan of the room. When his gaze landed on mine, he grinned and strolled deliberately toward me.

With each step he took, a nervous tickle jumped in my belly. By the time he reached me, it was like a swarm of grasshoppers bouncing off the walls of my stomach.

He slowed and dropped the notebook in front of me. "Hey." His lips quirked up in one corner.

"Hey."

My fingers fiddled with the pencil in my hands. The hat darkened the blue of his eyes, but there was no missing it. Zook Guthrie was hot as hell. Lord, give me strength.

Just tutoring.

"Did you get a new hat?"

"I did. Gen-u-wine Stetson." He adjusted it back and forth, but it landed in exactly the same position. "Felt. Better for the fall weather."

"It looks, um, really good on you." And it did. I'd never seen a sexier cowboy, even in the movies. "Did you practice your lettering?"

When I reached for the notebook our fingers touched. He kept his hand on mine and caught my gaze, focusing those baby blues all on me. Powder blue clouds surrounded his pupils and cobalt ringed the edges of his irises. Faint amber streaks twisted from top to bottom like the color trapped floating inside a marble. Gorgeous.

I coughed and opened the notebook. Flawless lettering filled every page, upper and lower case, front and back. "This is amazing."

"Ain't nuthin.'"

"Are you kidding me? Half the students here would kill to have penmanship like this. Precision is a rare skill. You'll learn fast. Sit. Please." I sat and looked up at him, but he didn't move. "You do want me to teach you now, right?"

"Yeah. I was just enjoying watching you getting all excited about that notebook. I can show you a few other things I'm really accurate at."

Oh my god. He didn't waste any time starting the flirting up again. I took a deep breath and tried to sound convincing. "Listen, Zook. Before we start. A few ground rules." One eyebrow rose and a corner of his mouth tipped up. "Just tutoring. No flirting. No inviting me back to your hotel. Strictly schoolwork, okay?"

By the time I finished my speech, both his eyebrows were up and his smirk had grown into a wicked smile. "Sure."

Dear lord, he did not sound like he meant that at all. Either way, I had him here, so I'd better make the best of it. "Let's finish up the alphabet and phonics. Then we'll put the letters together to make words."

"Alright." He pulled the chair out from the table and spread his legs wide as he sat down and leaned back. His posture was so manly and commanding, my eyes were drawn between his long legs.

"So, uh... We talked last time about *A*. Remember the bad avocado?"

"Yes." Was he smirking at our avocado joke or did he catch me staring at his belt buckle? A stunning gilded stallion rearing up on his hind legs.

I pointed to a row of perfect *B*s he'd lettered in the notebook. "And the *B* says *buh*, like *baby*."

His eyes teased me, but he didn't sing the song. He straightened up and forced his attention to the notebook. "*Buh*." He kept his voice flat. No jokes.

"Good. Let's carry on."

As we proceeded through the alphabet, he maintained his serious demeanor and picked up phonics easily. I kept expecting him to sing again. His lips twitched a few times, but he held back the obvious puns as we went through *O* and *P*.

"And the *Z* says *zzz* like zebra."

"*Zzz*."

"Excellent. Let's put it together now and do some CVC words."

"CeCe words?"

"Consonant-vowel-consonant."

"I like CeCe words better."

Okay, one joke in twenty-five minutes of hard work was forgivable.

"You'll sound out each letter and try to make a word. Try this one. *D-O-G*."

"D-oh-juh."

"If I told you *G* at the end this word makes the *guh* sound, how would you try again?"

"Doh-guh. Dog!"

"Yes! Write it down."

He lettered out *dog* on a sheet. "Dog."

"Dog," I repeated.

"I did it." He sounded surprised, but I expected he'd do well based on his lettering alone.

"I knew you could. You're smart. Just needed someone to sit down and take the time. One more..."

"I've got one." He poised his pencil and threw me a naughty wink. Oh boy.

"You do?"

With one elbow on the desk and his head down, he slowly wrote *S-E-X*. As he finished, he looked up at me with an adorable grin. "What's that spell?"

I giggled and looked around, as if anyone could see what he wrote. "Of all the words, this is the one you know?" I whispered.

"I know this word. Seems like people like to spell it out. I've never written it down before. Have you?"

"Have I what?"

"Written sex down?" His voice was deep and sexy and oh my, we'd just crossed a line from tutoring to flirting.

I fiddled with the button of my cardigan as the heat spread up my neck and burned in my cheeks.

"Do you have any more classes today?" he asked me.

"No."

"Let's go." He held out his hand, palm up, waiting for me to take it.

"Where?" I stared at his long fingers, the callouses on the pads beneath them, the wrinkle of his life line. Where would his life take him?

"Field trip," he answered.

I shook my head and looked at my lap to avoid his eyes. "No."

"No flirting. It's strictly educational."

"You promised to keep this platonic."

"It'll be completely chaste. I swear." He crossed his index and middle finger and placed them over his heart. "Totally nonsexual."

"I need to go." Gathering papers helped to distract me from his searching gaze. I tapped the stack on the desk a few too many times.

"You said you didn't have any classes."

Oh shoot. I did say that.

"I have to study. I forgot about a pop quiz tomorrow."

He grabbed the handful of pencils I was holding and slid off his chair, one knee bent. He tapped the eraser ends to an imaginary beat on the table. His lips sputtered, and strong puffs of air from deep in his throat made a syncopated "ch" sound.

"What're you doing?" A quick survey of the lobby showed the librarian wasn't looking and several students at the other desks hadn't noticed him. Yet.

He paused and smirked at me. "Beatbox."

"What?"

"Oh, Cecelia. I'm begging you please to come... come with me."

Okay. Despite the fact his voice and beatbox sounded incredibly good, the Hale Library was one of the most hallowed and historic places on campus. One did not sing songs in here or play beatbox with pencils.

"Oh my god. Stop."

My pleas only made him smile and project his voice more! *"Oh, oh, oh, oh..."* His percussion echoed through the lobby. Now he had the attention of the students and the librarian.

I leaned down so our faces were close and used my quiet-but-severe teacher voice. "Stop."

He laughed, pausing the ruckus for a moment. "Only if you come on a field trip with me."

I hesitated. He raised his pencils and took a deep breath, ready to belt out more *Oh*s.

"Alright. Okay. Just stop singing that horrible song."

"It's not horrible. It's a classic." He stood and handed me the pencils. I stuffed them in my bag, and he flipped his palm up as he had done before.

My *no* danced on the tip of my tongue. There was no way this could end innocently like he'd promised. But darn, when a man as insanely gorgeous and wickedly funny as Zook Guthrie holds out his hand for you, it's impossible not to take it.

His fingers closed around my palm like he'd done it a million times before. Firm, warm, comforting. Walking out of the library, the watching eyes made me nervous, but also proud and excited. Because the hottest cowboy on the planet was holding my hand and guiding me toward the door.

My phone. I needed to leave it here, or Maksim would see I'd gone outside my approved radius. Without Zook noticing, I slipped it between two books on the shelf closest to the exit. I'd have to come back tonight before the library closed to retrieve it.

Zook continued to hold my hand as we walked across the lawn to the library parking lot. He stopped at the first space, which had a motorcycle parked in it.

"That's our ride." He pointed to the bike. The navy-blue fuel tank and fenders reflected like they'd been recently shined.

"You bought a bike?"

"No, I bought a piece of crap Harley with a busted transmission and fixed her up." The bike wasn't like the shiny new crotch rockets you'd see around Hale in the spring. It was low to the ground, long, and wide. Zook detached a helmet from a lock under the seat and held it up between us. "This is gonna mess up your do."

Hmm. Having my body pressed up against Zook's? If I got away unseen, I could have the thrill of my life riding a motorcycle for the first time with a hot guy.

I grabbed the helmet and gripped it tight to my chest, feeling my pounding heart vibrate inside it. Glancing around, I didn't see Soraya or anyone who knew me. Would it be worth the huge risk to sit behind Zook and ride this bike?

He chuckled and swung one leg over the bike. Raising it up like a tripod, he looked at me. "Put it on then and get on." He angled his chin to the smooth passenger seat behind him. His charming smile, his pretty blue eyes, his wide back in his leather jacket. The decision was easy. Totally worth every second and any potential danger.

I shoved the giant helmet on my head. It felt heavy and swiveled loosely as I surveyed the cars in the lot again.

"Is there a problem?" he asked me.

"No, um. You don't have a helmet?"

"We ain't gonna crash."

"It's the law here. You must wear a helmet on a motorbike."

"Motorbike? Is that fancy talk for hog?"

"I think so. Whatever you call it, you are required to wear a helmet, or you'll be ticketed."

He glanced out of the lot to the street. "Are you sayin' you won't ride with me if I don't wear a helmet?" He grinned again, thinking he was sharing an inside joke with himself, but I was beginning to understand Zook's personality. He liked to tease and do it mercilessly.

"No. I'm saying it would be wise if you wore a helmet, even if the risk of crashing is minimal."

"Hmm-mmm." His tone made it clear we were talking about much more than head protection. "Is there a place in town I can get a helmet?"

"I believe there's an Army-Navy surplus. We might be able to purchase one there."

"Get on, then. We'll stop at the surplus and purchase a helmet for safety." He mocked my accent, but still, he had acceded to my request.

"Very well." I awkwardly swung a leg over and perched my fingertips on the outside of his jacket, making sure to keep an inch of distance between our torsos. Thank goodness I was wearing pants and boots today. My feet found the foot pegs and the soles of my boots slid around, finding a secure spot.

He rose up and I stared at his butt in his jeans as he cranked the kicker. God, what a beautiful view from right here.

The bike sputtered but didn't start. "Dammit." He jumped on it harder, giving it a full-strength kick. The engine rumbled to life against my legs. He settled in his seat and pulled my knees in so they hugged his hips. "Hold on!"

I gripped his sides more tightly.

"No. Like this." He took my wrists and yanked me forward. My chest hit his back, and he folded my hands over his belt buckle. "It's for your own safety." Heat from his body seeped through me like a newly lit match. My legs were forced open wide. The rough fabric of his jeans mashed against the crotch of my suede pants. I held back my groan at the wonderful sensations it caused. "Hold on tight, CeCe. You're going for a ride."

Bright sunbeams breaking through the trees forced me to blink. Zook's massive body warmed me against the chill. Gravity tried to pull me from my spot, but it failed. I'd never let go of my hold on Zook. We rolled out of the lot and out into the city, leaving Hale and all my worries behind.

Chapter 6

AFTER AN HOUR ON THE back of Zook's bike, my arms melded around his waist. My cheek found a resting place on his shoulder that put my mouth dangerously close to his ear. Good, so we could talk if we needed to—which we didn't often because we both got lost in the ride—but bad because each time he turned back to talk to me, our helmets crunched in a fiberglass kiss.

Zook handled the bike with the same precision as his lettering. I felt safe and secure pressed against his back. And free.

Free like the wind.

Zook could turn north and ride us to the Canadian border and I wouldn't stop him.

We reached Province Bluffs, home of America's most wealthy celebrities and politicians. Magnificent modern colonial estates passed us by in a blur. At the top of a sandy trail, in an area cleared of trees and bushes, he parked the bike and helped me off.

An enormous wooden frame of a house—no a mansion—rose from the ground, climbing up to the sky, but I couldn't look at the structure because the view mesmerized me. At the base of a steep cliff, the ocean crashed on the shore. I removed the helmet and crisp sea air assaulted me. "Wow."

"Welcome to mi humble casa."

We walked past a pile of supplies stacked in a corner and I stared up at the tall wooden spires. "It's so big."

"It is, and I'm not even hard right now."

"Huh?"

"Nothin."

I ignored his teasing to take in the grand entrance. Raw stairs climbed up to the sky like an Escher drawing. "Did you construct all this?"

"It's not done yet but yeah, what's here, I made."

"Is it going to be like the homes we saw on the way up?"

"Nope. Better. Let's sit." He moved aside a blue tarp hanging across one wall and revealed a small bedroom-like space with a twin mattress on the ground. He pulled a plaid blanket off from under some papers. He spread the blanket on the floor and motioned for me to sit next to him.

"So you're studying to be a teacher?" he asked as I settled next to him, leaving a safe distance between us.

"Yes."

"How many years you got left?"

"This is my last year. I'll earn my masters degree in June."

"And then you'll get some high-society teaching job?"

"Well, I'll try." Actually, I'll return to my prison of a home, and Maksim will brag about my degree. Most likely, I'll never teach a student apart from Zook and the kids in my student teaching program. I'd miss them all dearly.

"It's gonna be rough on your students," he said as if he was in my head.

"How so?" I said, testing him. There's no way he could know what I was thinking.

"The boys are gonna have crushes on you. They'll be hiding their boners behind their desks."

I laughed to shake off the thought he'd read my mind. Time to turn the attention back on him. "So, how'd you learn to build things?"

His teasing smirk flattened. He picked at a piece of fuzz on the blanket. "Not sure I'm ready to share the details with you."

Hmm. If he didn't want to tell me, I wanted to know. "You can trust me."

"Can I?" He looked up at me again with his sterling blue eyes. "Haven't trusted anyone since Van... Tessa."

"Why did you call her Van?"

"Oh man. See, that's why I can't talk about it. 'Cuz if I tell you where I'm from, Tessa's from the same place, and I'd be giving up her secrets too."

"Please." His gaze moved to my hand when I placed it on his. "I won't discuss it with anyone. I want to know more about you."

"Why?"

"You're interesting. Where does a man like you come from? Why were you never taught to read and write? Yet, you can build houses like this, and you make me laugh with a flick of your cowboy hat?"

He shook his head like I had it all wrong. "You do realize, after I tell you, you'll be so repulsed, you'll run down the streets of Province Bluffs screaming *there's a wacky dude building a house up there*!"

"I won't. Tell me. Don't I seem like someone you can trust?"

"You do. Alright then. You asked for it. Ever heard of Jebediah Bare-bones?"

"No, I don't recall hearing that name, but I heard you talking about someone named Jeb that night in the alley."

"Jeb Barebones is serving three life sentences in federal prison for murder and rape. He's Tessa's father."

"Oh." My hand flew to my lips to cover my open mouth.

"He was the leader of a break-off sect of a fundamentalist church. The man had thirty wives before the FBI took him down. Jeb Bare-bones dished out a doctrine of nutbag and his followers ate it up. He promised my parents eternal life, and they sacrificed their own children for it."

"You?

"Yes, me and my brother."

"Is his name Destry?"

"How did you... Oh that's right. Tessa asked me about him that first night. Destry's my only brother. Jeb cast him out and labeled him an apostate. He banned my dad from the church for supporting Destry. He split up my family. We never made contact again."

"What was it called?"

"The Brotherhood of God Church."

"So why'd you go to prison?"

"Federal jury convicted me of sexual assault."

My gasp came out louder than I intended. Zook didn't look like a violent man. More the opposite. His eyes were gentle, his movements slow and purposeful. "And um, was this related to the nutjob doctrine you mentioned?"

"I had sex with her. She didn't want it. Circumstances don't matter."

"But there were extreme circumstances?"

"Yes."

"Tell me."

"I did it because Jeb Barebones forced me to do it. He said he'd cast me out like Destry. He'd take me on a drive and drop me on the street with no money, a stupid kid who couldn't read."

"You're not stupid."

"That's not what he told me."

"So that scared you enough to make you do it?"

"Well that and his constant threats to kill my mother. Mom only produced two boys, so she was useless to him anyway. I fully believed he'd kill her like he murdered his own brother. I followed all Barebones' commands."

"Including raping a woman?"

"Yes. I spent a lot of time trying to earn his approval. By the time I did, he wanted me to *spread my seed* among the women of the church. I did everything I could to make it comfortable for her. Damn. It's pointless to talk about this because no matter what I say, I'm guilty. I'm not trying to justify what I did. I regret it. The worst mistake of my life. I'll never make it up to her." I could tell from the edge of desperation in his voice, this was torturing him.

"Have you spoken about it with anyone?"

"No. I plead guilty and they locked me up. End of story."

"It might be good for you to tell me. I promise I'll keep it between us, but you need to let this out."

His eyes considered me. He looked resigned, like he'd already told me so much, he might as well tell me the rest. "I was twenty-three. Old enough I shoulda had the balls to say no. There were rituals. Jeb had convinced the women they should cooperate. I always knew he was talking shit, but I was buying time, collecting evidence against him. My brother and I knew her. She was a nice girl. She did as she was told. I did as I was told. It was fast and I hope painless for her." He pulled on his hair and groaned.

"Zook. I understand. It happened to—I mean—I've read about this. When evil people have too much power, it's impossible to stand up to them. They threaten you with your worst fears."

"I shoulda let him cast me out. You know why? Because it happened anyway. Three weeks ago, the prison released me on the street. No money. No family. Threw me on a bus out of town. My worst fear came true. The kicker of it all? It's not that bad. Least I'm free. I learned from serving time. Fear makes a man weak. I'm not afraid of nothin' now, and I'm not weak anymore."

"No, you're not. You're very strong. I can see it. I feel it when I'm around you."

He nodded and stared over my shoulder like he was reliving the whole nightmare. "I provided evidence that got Barebones convicted of murder. Computers, pictures. When the trial came, the FBI had everything they needed. I nailed him. Doesn't make up for what I did, and the time I served doesn't take away the pain it caused her. I gotta live with that forever, but I did what I could to make it right."

Ocean waves cracked against the steep cliff below. The water receded with a sizzle, taking fragments of the cliff away with it, reshaping the shoreline one particle of sand at a time. Zook had been battered like a rocky bluff at the edge of a tumultuous sea. If only I could be half as brave as him and face the storms ahead of me.

The talk of his past was upsetting us both. A change in topic was needed. "So how is this a field trip for our tutoring sessions?"

"Hmm?" He snapped out of it and turned his attention back to me. A small smile grew on his lips, like looking at me made him happy.

He reached back and grabbed the oversized roll of papers from the top of his bed. The edges of the plans curled into his palm like he'd spent hours looking at them.

"You read plans?"

"I can read the numbers or guess close enough." He pointed to a small boxed area of notes in the bottom left corner of the front page. "What's this say?"

"*Gunmetal gray Tuscan marble tiles supplied by Neptune Rock Quarry, New York.*"

"Ah, see, the owner said all my materials would be in the yard. I'm sure there's no Italian tile in my supplies. I need to order it."

"Can you call him?"

"I'd rather solve problems on my own as they come up. Trying to prove myself. He gave me a credit card."

"Do you have a phone?"

"Yeah. He gave me a business phone too. Nice guy. Not sure why he took a chance on me, but I'm not gonna let him down. I need to get that stone here pronto if I'm gonna have this place finished on time."

"How long do you have?"

"Till June. Nine months. Three of those are winter months, which is more like one regular month if Mother Nature cooperates, which she usually doesn't."

"You'll have strong winds up here on the bluffs when the nor'easters blow through."

"Wind and rain are my enemies. And snow. Shit. I need to get a plow. No way I can shovel a lot this big and get the work done. If I miss the deadline, I'm fired. My first chance at making my first mil ruined."

"Your first mil?"

"See, I gotta plan. One million my first year out of prison."

"Wow."

"Been poor long enough. My turn to be rich. Looks like my boss Torrez has the means to get me started. Then I'll take it from there."

"I believe in you." He smiled and my stomach flipped. Time to change the subject again. "How many bedrooms is this place going to have when you're done?"

The papers crackled as he flipped through them again. "Fifteen bedrooms, all with en suite baths, grand dining room, restaurant-grade kitchen. The whole basement will be set up as a gym. That's just the interior. Outside there's tennis courts, pools, stables, and a mother-in-law's quarters. It'll look like a huge castle on a cliff. Turrets and everything."

"Sounds fantastic."

He closed the plans and set them aside. He gazed into my eyes with his lips in a slight smirk. A breeze blew through the open space, tightening the air between us and raising little bumps on my arms. Zook's intention showed in his eyes. No more talking. He inched his head closer to mine, leaning forward on his palm. I had no choice. He was too beautiful to fight. The universe wanted me to kiss him.

He slanted his head and pressed his lips to mine. A flurry of sparks ignited in my tummy and between my legs. His fingertips scrunched the hair at my nape. He felt it too. Pure fireworks. We opened our mouths at the same time, our lips racing to get closer. More. More. More.

He needed it. I had to have it. What was this foreign feeling inside me? I knew.

For the first time in my life, I felt wanted.

All I ever wanted.

Desired. And being desired by a man as gorgeous as Zook made it so much better than I'd dared to dream.

I whimpered because it hit me too deep. It felt so good, I never wanted him to stop. He grunted in response, and with his hand supporting my neck, he lowered me to my back on the blanket. When he moved on top of me, we fit together like lock and key. Hot trails scorched my skin where his hands skimmed my sides, over my breasts, and into my hair.

Our hips rubbed together and I moaned. "Oh my god!"

"Amen," he murmured into my neck. His hips pressed against my core through our clothes and I could feel how much he wanted me. I was losing control. This could easily escalate to hot, naked sex in seconds. But that couldn't happen. *Platonic. Too risky.*

I tore my lips from his and gasped. He stared at me with question in his hooded eyes. Man, Zook's eyes glowed an even brighter blue when he was turned on. "We should stop."

"We should go. You ever had a kiss like that before?"

"Not even close."

"Then we shouldn't stop. We've barely scratched the surface. Let me show you."

Oh god, yes. I wanted that. More than anything. But... "I haven't... I mean..."

He raised up on his elbows to stare down at me. "Are you a virgin?"

"No."

"Why stop?" He pulled his torso away and oxygen flowed back to my brain. What should I tell him?

"I'm not experienced." This was true. Not the reason I was stopping though.

"But you're not a..." His eyebrows rose. "Have you ever had an orgasm before?"

I shook my head. "No. I don't think so. And the way you made me feel... This is very overwhelming."

"Alright." He sucked in a long breath and ran his hand through his hair. He slid off me and smiled. "We'll stop. But you know you just challenged me."

"I didn't." I sat up and pulled my sweater tight around me.

"Oh you did. The student gets to teach the teacher. And I know a lot of things that will blow your mind."

"Oh my." That sounded lovely.

"But if you want to stop now, I respect that."

I didn't want to stop. I needed to. This could not happen.

He swung his leg around and tucked my back up to his chest, wrapping his arms around my midsection. A rod as big as a soda can nudged my spine as we cuddled. He might as well have kept kissing me because this felt even more intimate.

Talk. Talk would be good about now. I needed to say... anything.

"Why did you never learn to read? I mean I know you worked as a child and didn't go through formal schooling, but there's a certain amount of learning that happens by association and osmosis. Like the word sex. You knew how to spell that and wrote it fairly easily."

His forehead pressed against the back of my head and tension oozed off him. I knew it would be hard for him to answer, but I needed to know how a man as smart as him could go so long without learning to read.

"Pure bull-headed stubbornness. Very few people actually knew. I can cover pretty well."

"You sure do. I never would've guessed."

"If someone did figure it out and wanted to help, like Tessa, I'd shut them down or distract them with jokes before they got started."

"But you let me tutor you?"

"Yes."

"So what changed? It can't all be me."

"You were a huge part of it. But... prison changes a man. Made friends with a guy, Gustavo, he was a street fighter. We fought back whenever anyone came after us. He'd take my back. I took his."

"Did Gus get out too?"

"Not yet. He had another year. But he taught me more than fighting. He taught me we only got one shot at this life, and it might be short. So I vowed, if I got out, I'd make something of myself."

"You're doing that."

"Yeah." He was quiet for a moment then said, "But don't underestimate the power of a tight sweater over your tempting rack. I wanted to fuck your brains out so bad, I was like *teach me, baby*."

I laughed and turned to look at him over my shoulder. "Shall we go now?"

"No. Let's sit a minute. Don't know when I'll have a beautiful girl up on the bluffs again. Want to savor it."

I gave him my weight and sank deeper into his warm embrace. I closed my eyes and smiled. When I was with Zook, my worries disappeared. His kisses tasted divine. He was funny and sweet and so handsome. I wasn't lying when I told him it was an honor to be his tutor. If only I didn't have to return to Veranistaad after graduation.

Veranistaad. No. Oh god. What had I done? I couldn't cuddle with a man on a bluff!

If Maksim found out, he'd make good on his threats to kill me and anyone I cared about.

No, I had to follow the rules. I would return to my fake marriage, and the role I played as "princess."

His arms locked around me when I made to get up and run.

"Hey. What's wrong, princess?"

"Prin... You..." Oh gosh. Seriously? Of all the endearments, he picked this one for me?

Whatever. I needed to get out of here. Except I was an hour's motorcycle ride from campus. An hour pressed to his back. An hour to fabricate a lie to get rid of him. I'd have to hurt him. If I didn't, nothing would prevent me from falling deeply in love with Zook Guthrie.

I tried to stand again and he let me this time. The confusion on his face broke my heart.

"I forgot. I really do need to get back to campus." The first lie of many I'd have to tell him to keep us both safe.

THE JOY I'D FELT RIDING up the hill turned to suffocating fear on the ride back to Hale. Zook must have sensed it because he kept pressing his hand over mine at his belt buckle, gently wrapping my arm tighter around him. By the time we arrived back at the library parking lot, I'd rationalized waiting till after the next tutoring session. That way I could give him the study materials he needed to carry on without me.

We got off the bike and I gave him my helmet. He pulled his off and smiled at me. "I'd like to see you again, CeCe."

I shook my head.

"You nervous about being with an ex-con?"

"That's not it." I didn't want him to think that.

"Whatever's making you hold back, I want you to know you're safe with me." He held my cheeks in his palms. "You don't need to be scared. We can go at whatever speed you like as long as it's not backwards."

God, why did he have to be so sweet? If I could date Zook, those words would make me feel so comfortable. But no...

I let him kiss me. I kissed him back like it was our last kiss. Which it was. He responded by deepening the kiss. I forced myself to pull away first.

"Goodbye, Zook."

"You okay getting home?"

"Yeah, I have to review some notes, and then I have a car here." And I need to get my phone from where I'd stashed it in the library.

"I'll see you next Monday for tutoring."

I nodded. Yes, one last time.

Chapter 7

ZOOK

"I've got a joke for you this time."

Oh, CeCe was going to try her hand at humor.

"Hit me." I tapped the desk and smiled at her.

"What does a cyclops' Valentine's Day card say?"

God, she's cute when she's playful like this. "I don't know."

"Eye love you." She pointed to the center of her forehead and widened her eyes. "Get it? Eye love you."

"Oh, I get it. And eye," I pointed to my forehead, "love you too."

We both had huge grins as we stared at the other pointing to our foreheads. Our hands slowly lowered and the smiles faded. We'd said *I love you* to each other. Even if it was a joke, it felt good to say it to her. I could love her. Easily. And soon. Very soon. And she could love me too. It's in her eyes. She's crazy about me.

"This will be our last session," she said.

Or she could slice my heart to shreds with an axe.

"Why's that?"

"You've made good progress. You can carry on on your own. I've prepared a self-study guide for you." Lying to me again. I was nowhere near ready to teach myself. She twisted the pendant necklace resting near her throat, a sure sign of deception.

"Is this about me kissing you?"

"No."

"You got issues dating a man who ain't rich? Yet. I say yet, CeCe, because it won't be long. This project is the first of many, and I got plans to go big. Soon."

"It's not that." Her voice trembled, no conviction in her tone. "We just... It's time to end it." My gut told me this wasn't about money or me being an ex-con. The connection we had scared her shitless. She'd never had anything like this. Shoot, it intimidated me, and I had a lot more experience than her. She just needed some time to get to know me. I'd given up trying to get her in bed. Now I wanted her trust.

"Shame. I had an excellent date planned for this weekend."

Her eyes opened wide and a smile sneaked at the corners of her lips. "Really? Where?"

Oh excellent. She liked surprises. "Someplace really cool. But if we're ending things. Well, I'll just cancel it."

She crossed her arms over her chest and sulked. "Tell me what you had planned."

"First, promise me you'll go."

She pressed her lips together and looked around.

"Don't make me start singin' your song here in the library again."

"I- I'll go." She spoke quickly. "One date."

"Oh, there will be many dates."

"No. Just this one, okay?"

"Sure." Whatever she needed to tell herself, I'd go along. But I liked being with her, looking at her, kissing her. There would be many dates.

"What did you have planned?"

"Here's a clue. You'll need this." I pulled a black beret with a hot pink feather out of my backpack and plopped it on her head. Cute. CeCe made any ridiculous outfit work. "You have to wear it Friday. We're taking my bike, so wear a really short skirt."

"Wouldn't it ride up?"

"Yes." I dragged the word out, waiting for her to catch up.

"Oh." She giggled and there it was, the blush on her neck where her pendant hung. I'd stared at that spot for hours. Needed to get my mouth on this woman again.

"Program your address in my phone. I'll pick you up Friday night at six." I held out my phone.

"Oh. Hmm."

"You have a problem with me seeing your place?"

She bit her lip. "No. It's fine." She typed in her address and handed it back to me. "Here."

"Good." I tucked the phone in my pocket. "Now you have more jokes or you wanna teach me some more words that don't sound like they're spelled?

"I don't have any more jokes."

"Then let's get down to business."

FRIDAY NIGHT, I PARKED the bike in front of a townhouse in an affluent neighborhood near Hale. Her front door was two fucking stories tall. I rapped the huge hanging knocker. A girl who was not Cecelia opened the door. A pretty girl with black hair. Shit. The girl from Siege.

"Hi." Her gaze swept up and down my body. She smiled like she approved of what she saw. I was wearing a pair of charcoal slacks and a slate gray button-down shirt under my motorcycle jacket. My Stetson was in the carrying compartment of the bike, and I had my hair slicked back.

"I'm Soraya." Around her neck, she wore the same pendant necklace I'd seen on Cecelia.

"Pleasure." I tipped my head. "Zook."

"I know. She told me. She said you're a pretty darn good kisser too."

"Did she now?" She'd been gabbing about me to her roomie. Good news.

"Where are you guys going?" she asked, leaning a shoulder against the open door.

"Do you believe in magic, Soraya?"

She stood up straight. "I do."

"Is he here?" CeCe came up behind her and locked eyes with me over Soraya's shoulder. "Hi," she said, breathy and smiling.

God, she looked gorgeous. Short black skirt as I instructed, but with black leggings to keep her warm on the bike. High heeled boots up to her knees, tight pink sweater with the top two buttons open. And the black beret with the pink feather. My girl was good at following directions.

"Hey, babe. Grab your jacket."

Cecelia brushed past Soraya. I took her hand and planted a kiss on her lips.

Soraya's grin grew bigger. "Have fun, you two."

I tugged Cecelia down the steps to the curb where my bike was waiting. I waved back at Soraya. Cecelia giggled as she slipped on her helmet. Oh yeah, she was excited.

My hands guided her into her place behind me. "Hold on, babe. Ride of your life coming up."

She wrapped her arms tight and sighed. As the wind whipped our faces, I realized. This felt right. Cecelia on the back of my bike, her thighs squeezing my hips. No place else I'd rather be.

<hr>

"FOR MY NEXT ILLUSION, my magic wand will select two suckers... I mean participants from the audience." The magician had CeCe laughing and staring with her mouth open for ten minutes already with his card tricks and mind reading.

"Here it goes. Watch closely." He tossed his wand into the air. The crowd mumbled *ooo* and *ahh* as it floated over to CeCe and me. It hovered above our heads for a moment, then changed course. It looked like it would pick another couple, only to come back to us. The wand lowered and tapped the pink feather in her hat. It tapped my head next.

"C'mon up, folks. My wand has selected you, and it is never wrong."

We walked up on stage, and the magician explained how he would transport us like Dorothy through a cyclone to the Land of Oz. "Climb in, my friends. Don't be afraid. I promise not to lose you to the munchkins."

We stepped into the box.

"Face each other and hold hands." I liked this guy. I'd gladly hold her hands. The bottom of the box lowered like an elevator to an even smaller cube, forcing us closer together. Yep, I liked this guy.

"Change clothes," a woman under the stage whispered urgently.

"What?"

"Exchange your tops. The joke is you went through a cyclone."

"I'm not wearing no girl clothes."

"It's part of the act. Take off your shirt."

Wait. If I had to take off mine, she had to take off hers. I suppose I could suffer a little humiliation for that. I unbuttoned my shirt and slipped it off.

"Oh my god!" CeCe covered her gaping mouth with her hands, her eyes wide.

"What?"

"I didn't know you were so cut under there. You're gorgeous. All lean muscle. Holy cow!" She squeezed my biceps and ran her fingers down my arms. All the work I'd put in at the gym in the slammer and working hard on the house paid off right now. She licked her lips as she took me in. This could all be yours, baby. Just stop with the resisting act.

"What's this tattoo?" Her fingers traced the treble clef and blank music staff over my left pec.

"Long story."

"Hurry, hurry!" The woman giving instructions couldn't see us through the walls. As the crowd laughed above us, the box started to move sideways, and I steadied her with our joined hands.

The draw between us exploded in the confined space. The overwhelming need to kiss her consumed me. "We have to switch," I said, my throat tight. "Give me your sweater."

"Oh, um..." She started on her top button. I'd dreamed of this many times. Although usually I tore the buttons, but watching her delicate fingers do it worked too. She slipped off her sweater, and I was right. A fancy bra made her boobs look like candy. A beautiful round candy I had to eat right now. Screw the show. They could open this box with us fucking on the inside. My mouth hit the swells of her breasts and kissed them. Soft, hard, round. Smelled like oranges. Better than candy. She gasped and grabbed my head, pulling me in. Yes!

"Are you ready? It's almost time!" the woman outside the box screeched.

I forced my face from her cleavage and kissed her lips. "Jesus, CeCe. You're driving me loony here. We gotta go out on stage and I'm sporting a woody."

She giggled, which didn't help my situation. "Put it on." She pressed her pink sweater to my chest. "I don't see how it'll fit you."

The box stopped moving as I struggled to find the sleeves of her sweater. My shirt covered her completely. Good, 'cuz I'd never let her go on stage wearing that bra. My forearms stuck midway through the sleeves of her sweater. I managed to get one button closed by stretching it to the max. I didn't want to rip it, so my chest and abs were on full display.

"You look ridiculous." She pressed her lips together, trying to stop her laughter. "And hot."

"Ready or not, you're going up!" the woman warned. The box lifted us back to the stage level.

"And here they are, ladies and gentlemen. Our transported couple. Safe and sound."

The door opened and the lights shined on us. The crowd went nuts. The magician held our hands up, showing more of my body. Women whistled and hooted.

"Well, it appears the tornado has messed with their clothes. The trick didn't work out exactly as planned, but hey, look at the hot guy wearing a pink sweater."

The crowd cheered again. Someone called, "Take it off!"

The magician held up his hands to silence the crowd and turned his attention to me. "Did you get your heart?"

I nodded.

"Did you get your brain?"

CeCe nodded like she knew the script.

"Great! Apart from the wardrobe malfunction, the illusion was a success! They have been to Oz and found their true desires were within them from the beginning. Thank you for being good sports. And thank you for those abs." He waved his hand with his little finger perched up. Oh man, no wonder this guy was so eager to set the trick up for me. "You may go backstage and change clothes."

We waved to the applauding crowd and exited the stage, both laughing like crazy fools. In a corner dressing room, I took off her sweater and handed it back to her. "This was very unfair. You're all covered up."

"I think the ladies in the audience enjoyed seeing your six-pack. And a few of the men. The magician was totally checking you out."

"Oh yeah?" I wrapped my arms behind her back and pulled her close. "Give me my shirt back." I waggled my eyebrows because she was wearing my shirt, and I'd get to see her bra again.

When she stepped back, she hunched her shoulders and looked down.

"Shy all of a sudden? You had no problem in the box."

"We had to do what they said in time or we'd ruin the trick."

"So you won't undress for me unless a magician is forcing you to do it? You can go behind that screen and change. I won't force you to do anything."

"I know." As she worked the buttons of my shirt, her breasts came into view again. Her tits and her expensive bra looked even more tempting in the bright lights. It was pale-pink lace, to match her sweater. If she was into matching, her panties would be black to match her skirt and tights, or would she go pink to match her top?

She handed me the shirt and stood before me in her bra.

"Absolute perfection."

I took her in my arms again. Her breasts pressed up against my bare chest nearly did me in. "Did you enjoy the show?"

"Yes! So much! You planned it?"

"I arranged for him to ask you on stage. He added my part in the act and the nudity, but I'll take the way it turned out." I planted my lips on hers, and she kissed me back.

My still-hard dick twitched. "Now, I don't wanna create a scene here in the dressing room, so we'd better head out."

"Okay."

Chapter 8

THE FALL CHILL HELPED calm my boner as we strolled the colonial streets of Boston.

"How's the mansion coming along?" she asked.

"Fast. The floors and walls are in. Part of the roof. Wanna come see it?"

"Yes."

We hopped on my bike and drove out to Province Bluffs.

"Cold?" I helped her get her helmet off. The leggings under her skirt and short jacket didn't look thick enough. We needed to get her a motorcycle jacket. She'd look hot in leather pants to match.

"No." She removed the band from her ponytail and shook her hair out. Beautiful. "You kept me warm." Her eyes scanned the house. Drywall was up. Most of the roof was done. Still looked like a shithole. "Wow! It looks amazing."

"It doesn't yet. But it will. Trying to finish the roof before the first snowfall."

"Do you have anyone helping you?"

"Torrez, my boss, gave me a four-man crew. I could use fifty, but if I make it with a small crew, he'll be more impressed. Subcontractors will help out with landscaping and electrical. I just need to supervise and coordinate. I'm doing most of it myself because I want to make sure it's done right."

"Did the tile arrive?"

"Yep. High-quality stuff. It'll look good. Come on. I'll show you the best part."

Her cute butt bobbed in my face as she climbed the spiral staircase off the entry. She shimmied through the crawlspace in the third-floor ceiling into a room only five feet in diameter. Just enough for two people.

"What's this? An attic?"

"A turret. Look out the window." I didn't have the glass in yet, so the cold air blew her hair back as she leaned on the sill. I'd worked like a bat outta hell to finish the roof in here for tonight. She stiffened when I wrapped an arm around her waist and tucked her into my chest, but I pressed my lips to her neck and she relaxed. The curve of her ass fit right into my hips.

"It's stunning." She placed her hand on top of my arm. The moon put on a supreme show for me, making the waves a fluorescent white.

With my nose nuzzling her hair, I spoke softly in her ear. "I don't have much to offer you right now, CeCe. That's gonna change. Soon. But until then, I can give you this. The edge of the Atlantic."

Her head lowered as I spoke.

"Think of how wondrous it is. From here, there's miles of water with no land. The whales are their kings. Mother Nature is their god. Our world is inconsequential to them."

A hiccup rocked through her shoulders as she covered her face with her hands.

"What's wrong?"

"Nothing."

Shit. I'd made her cry. "You don't like my free gift?"

"I love it. You'll never know how much."

I spun her shoulders and caught her gaze. My carefully put together Cecelia—her makeup smudged under her eyes, her hair a mess from the helmet and the wind—looked incredibly vulnerable and utterly gorgeous. "Why does the ocean make you cry?"

"I bet you can see lots of migrating birds from here."

She never answered me when I asked her a direct question. Alright. I'll play along. "You like to watch birds?"

"Yes."

"Why?"

She shook her head and sniffled. Her fingers swiped at her face, smearing the black more, adding more perfect imperfection.

"Tell me about the birds."

"You know. They just... form flocks. They join together for a common goal, flying over us in a V formation. Winter is inevitable. They can't stay where they are, so they flap their wings and go somewhere they'll be happy and the sun will shine."

A loose lock of her hair flapped in the wind and stuck to her face. "And you wish you could fly away?" I smoothed it down her cheek and tucked it behind her ear.

"Yes." She huffed a nervous laugh. "Don't we all?"

"Uh-huh." I wasn't sure what she wanted me to say, but her eyes were begging me to kiss her.

When my hand wrapped in her hair, she arched her neck for me. She tasted warm and sugary like last time, but more desperate. I gave her all I could in that kiss. With a nip at her bottom lip, she opened her mouth and our tongues tangled. What were we talking about? I didn't know. All I knew was she needed to get naked so I could slam my dick inside her.

No, no, no. Slowly, carefully, gently. I had to break through to her little by little. A jackhammer would only scare her away.

I guided her back against the wall and smashed my body along the length of hers.

She moaned. Her fingers crawled through the short hair on the back of my head and latched onto the longer part at the top.

"Yes, baby." I encouraged her. "Let go."

She sucked in my kisses like she'd been underwater without air for hours and my lips were an oxygen ventilator. Whatever she needed, my mouth provided.

I'd been pressing my hands to the wall behind her head, trying to control myself, but when her hips surged out and ground against my cock through our clothes, all that blew out the open window. My hands flew to her breasts, clasping them from below and pushing them up. I kissed down her neck and lavished the swells of her boobs with kisses.

She pushed me away and stared into my eyes. And as I looked at her through my passion-hazed gaze, she changed.

Damn. Damn. Damn. Too fast.

A dark veil closed over her face. The switch flipped inside her.

I lost her eyes as she dropped to her knees and—what the fuck?—worked open my belt buckle. As she started on the button, her smile faded and her hands faltered. What the hell was this?

She acted... obligated. She'd gone submissive on me. My sexy tutor transformed into my servant. All wrong. I'd seen too many women kneeling to men back home. Women should stand and men should worship. Women are strong, and we are stupid ogres compared to them.

Even though my dick was about to burst free on its own, I reached down and pulled her up with my hands under her arms. "Stand up, darlin."

Wide, vacant eyes stared back at me. "I thought... Isn't that what you want? Don't you want me to please you?"

"I do when it's right, but something's off. Let me take care of you first." Talking was not gonna work now because my head was in my pants, and she was lost in her own head. I knew one surefire way to get through to her. "Rest against the sill." She leaned her elbows on the window sill, and I kissed her lips.

As I worked open the buttons of her sweater, the alluring candy from earlier came into view again. I trailed my lips down her neck, kissing every inch of newly exposed skin. With each kiss, her muscles relaxed. "This here." I pressed my lips to the top of her cleavage and skimmed the tip of my nose out to one nipple, gave it a gentle nip, and returned to the other one. "This is so magnificent. Any man would give his last dollar to be where I am right now."

Slowly, my Cecelia came back to me. I took my time working off her leggings and skirt, enjoying each new morsel of her exposed skin. Yep, I was right. Pink underwear matching the lacy bra. I inhaled with my nose hovering over her belly button. "God, you smell so good. I could play here all night kissing the curves and dips, smelling you. It's like citrus. It's mesmerizing."

My fingers tugged the panties down her hips, and my mouth followed. I lifted her knee to work them over her foot. I kissed behind her knee, opening her up to me. "This is where I belong. Between your legs, looking at your sweet pussy." She tensed and moved her leg in slightly to obscure my view. "Relax. Let me do this. Feel my lips. My breath. The pure heat between us." I scaled my mouth down to her core and rested my lips just over her clit. "Let it take over. Don't fight it."

I licked her once, nice and gentle.

"Oh god." She arched her back and gripped my hair.

"Feel good?"

"Yes."

"More?"

"Ugh!"

"I'll take that as a yes."

My lips closed around her clit and sucked. I ran my mouth down and tasted her. Sweet honey coated my tongue. "Damn, girl. Tastes so good." I wanted to stay there forever.

"Please... I can't."

"You can. Let me show you. Relax. Feel this." I lapped at her clit and sucked. She writhed and squirmed as I worked two fingers inside her soaking wet pussy. Her breathing sped up and her hips spasmed. "That's it. Good."

She froze and held her breath. With a throaty moan, her soft core gripped my fingers tight, clenching over and over. It went on forever. Heavy breaths gushed out of her, and her clit pulsed on my tongue.

Damn. Beautiful. Hot as hell.

I kissed back up her tummy to her lips. She attacked me again with a hungry kiss. Her hand landed on my dick and squeezed. Not submissive anymore. Aggressive. She wanted it. And damn I did too. I groaned into her mouth.

"Let me help you." She rubbed her hand over my erection.

"I can wait." I nuzzled her ear with my nose. My dick might self-combust but if she needed me to wait, I could do that.

"No." She had my pants undone and reached inside my briefs to grab my cock.

"Holy shit." I sucked in a breath through my teeth as delicate fingers wrapped around my dick and squeezed. It had been too damn long since anyone's hand except my own had been there.

"Oh my god. It's so big."

I couldn't answer her. I was too busy biting my lip to stave off a very premature ejaculation. Cecelia wearing nothing but her pink bra, her face flushed from her orgasm. Her hand stroked up and down once. "That feels fucking incredible."

My words spurred her on, and she went to town. Our lips crashed together as she pumped my cock like she was trying to get water from a dried up well.

My hips thrust back. We were lost in the moment and in each other. Too soon, a wall of pleasure surged from my balls and I came hard. My come hit the other wall of the turret, I shot so far.

Holy fuck, so damn good.

She kept pumping. Milking every last drop out of me. Cecelia was going to be the death of me.

"Come here." I wrapped her in my arms and turned us so my back was to the wall.

"Was that your first orgasm?" I asked her.

"Yes."

"Good. Happy to give you that."

"Mmm."

"One thing, CeCe. When you're with me—each and every time—you will be pleased before me. At least once. With you tasting this good, I'm thinking twice before I sink my dick into you."

She gasped and her head popped up. "We're not going to do it."

With my hand on her head, I brought her ear to rest on my pec. "Mmm-hmm. Not gonna argue with you right now because I'm liking the way you're looking all relaxed in my arms. Enjoying that. We'll talk about fucking some other time after I get a better sense of what's ticking in your head. Right now I just wanna hold you."

"Okay."

"Are you tutoring me Monday?"

"Yes." She dragged it out like it was obvious.

"You're done trying to end our sessions?"

"Unequivocally." She sighed and snuggled her head up under my chin.

"What's that mean?"

"Without question."

"Ha!" I squeezed her tight. "My new secret weapon. Whenever CeCe starts giving me *no, we shouldn't*, I make her come hard and it's *yes, no questions asked*."

She giggled for a long time. She shivered in the cold.

"Let me take you downstairs."

"Okay."

I helped her dress and guided her to the room I was using as a bedroom. I sat on the floor in front of my mattress and pulled her down between my legs, her back to my front.

"Can I ask you a question?" She twisted and peered up at me.

"No."

She punched my chest. "C'mon."

"Okay. What is your question, Cecelia?"

"The Brotherhood was a strict religion, right? They must've kept things from you."

"Mmm-hmm."

"How do you know so much?"

"Like how to make you come hard with my magical tongue?"

"Yeah. And like the song. Simon and Garfunkel? How do you know that?" She pulled away and turned to look at me. I kept a hand on her knee, not ready to lose contact just yet.

"I was away on jobsites a lot. Jeb couldn't enforce his rules when we were off the compound. My brother and I went nuts trying to find stuff. We'd watch TV and radio in hotels or on our phones. You tell teenage boys they can't do something, they'll find a way to do it. Every chance we got, we'd go out cruising for girls. Destry was a chick magnet."

"Your brother? I'm sure you were too."

"Yeah, wasn't too hard to meet girls. Anyway, when I was chosen by the prophet, Jeb brought me into the inner circle. What a fucking double standard. The men could do what they wanted. The women were isolated and secluded. He'd take me up into his private room for men only. He had TV, radio, internet, magazines with pictures of naked women. Porn videos. It was weird, but I got an education on that part of life at least, even if nobody was teaching me to read."

"So you learned about sex from porn?"

"Nah. Mostly from times out with Destry. And Vanity, during the time I was with her."

"Did you guys do it a lot?"

"Vanity? No. We didn't do it. Back on the compound, you couldn't get away with anything. Jeb had eyes everywhere. We managed to take the horses out before everyone woke up, but we never had much privacy. The one time I pushed it... It was her eighteenth birthday. Jeb caught us. Punished her bad. Sent me away. That was the last I saw her before she escaped and Jeb made me go with him after her."

"What happened?"

"He said I had to go with him to Boston. Said he found Vanity and she needed to be brought home."

"So you did it?"

"I wanted to be there as a witness so I could testify against him if he hurt her."

"So how did Jeb get arrested?"

"Vanity and Rogan fooled him into confessing. By then I had all the evidence I needed against Jeb, so I cooperated. I was too late. I'll never forgive myself for not stepping up sooner. I was so blinded by fear, I let Jeb dictate everything."

"I know how that is."

"Do you?"

"Yeah."

"Tell me." I knew she wouldn't, but I asked anyway.

"You know that first night when you fought with Rogan and Dallas?"

I chuckled at her sneaky change of topic. "Yeah?"

"I thought you were incredibly brave. And hot. Like really hot."

"You did?"

"I was shocked you fought back against two big guys. Even when they pulled a gun on you, you didn't back down."

"Mmm."

"And when you looked at me, bumps formed on my skin and my spine tingled. In a really good way."

"Thank you for covering for me."

"I don't even know why I said it was my drink. My gut told me I should."

"It wasn't your drink?" I asked.

"No. Rogan assumed it was, and I didn't have the courage or desire to correct him."

"I thought it was your drink. Was hoping you'd come back. Wasn't hoping to get caught though."

"Must've been a rough time for you."

"I shouldn't have done it. It was my first night in town. I didn't have any money, no place to stay."

"Where did you end up staying that night?"

Oh shit. More reasons for her to run. "You want the truth?"

"Yes, please tell me."

"I didn't have money for a motel room. I thought I might be sleeping under a bridge."

"Oh no."

"I ended up walking the streets of Boston trying to figure out where the bums hung out. In an alley in a bad neighborhood, I witnessed a drug deal going down. The supplier pocketed a bunch of cash and the buyer walked away. It was just me and him in that alley. I knew he had cash and he was a dealer."

"So what did you do?"

"I jumped him. He put up a good fight, but no one can beat me. Took the cash. A thousand bucks. Managed to lift his gun too."

"You attacked a drug dealer and took his gun?"

"Yeah."

"Oh my god. You're crazy."

"A little. We all are. Slept in a motel that night though. Had enough money to buy your damn golden goose coffee and pooshootoe."

"Prosciutto." She corrected me.

"Whatever." I turned her around and settled her back against my chest. "And, babe."

"Yeah?"

"I'll let it go this time. But you will tell me what you fear. Hear me?"

She tensed and answered quietly. "Okay."

Yeah, she was gonna need a lot more orgasms before she'd tell me. Fine with me.

Chapter 9

I WAS WORKING ON THE third downstairs bathroom. Torrez knocked on the open door. I put down my wrench and looked up at him from behind a toilet. He had a set of plans in one hand and some beautiful woman on his left. Great. Gave her a good view of my plumber's crack. I washed my hands and shook his.

"Lavonte."

"Guthrie."

"This is my right-hand man, Blythe."

"Pleasure to meet you, ma'am." I tipped my hat to her.

"I'm no ma'am and no man. I'm a woman and I know you both know that by the way you're staring at my tits, so let's get real about it."

"My apologies." One thing I'd mastered was kissing ass with a charming smile.

"Accepted." She returned a brief grin and piped down.

"How do you like it so far?" I asked Torrez.

"Looks pretty good. You did all this with four men?"

"Working day and night on my own. It's a big fucking place, but I'll get it done."

"Let's walk it."

Shit. A surprise inspection. I had nails everywhere, sawdust on the floor, pipes laying around.

I walked him through the area I'd finished up front. The stairs to the turret, a guest bedroom, and guest bath.

"The entry and stairs look perfect. Fine workmanship."

"Woodwork's my specialty."

He inspected the shower head in the guest bathroom.

"The plans call for dual thermodynamic waterfall rain shower heads. How many have you done so far?"

"Just this one. It's temporary so I could use it. I'll get the fixtures sorted later."

"You'll need to replumb it. The waterfall pipes in from the roof. The body massage sprays need a dedicated line in the walls."

"Alright."

He rolled the plans out on the bathroom counter. "See it here on the plans?"

"Yep."

"This tub should have LED lights."

"I can add those."

"Read this to me. What does it say?"

"I don't have my glasses."

"Can you read, Zook?"

I didn't answer.

"You did all this and you can't read?"

"Got a really good tutor."

"Impressive. Well done, Zook."

My favorite words. A job well done. I'll take it.

"Blythe will be dropping by to read the plans to you," Torrez announced like he was my father, which he wasn't. I didn't take orders from no one.

"I don't need no help. I can read the drawings."

"I'm aware of that. But if you want to get this done on time, you'll need to read the notes right the first time. There's no time for do-overs. Let her help."

"I'll come by on Saturday morning. Does that work for you?" Blythe asked.

"Sure." Mornings to a woman like her meant ten a.m. I'd already have six hours in by then.

"I'll just go over the details with you and leave you to your work."

That would be good. I didn't need no woman checking in on me like a mom.

We walked toward the front door. Torrez pulled out a gun. I jumped back with my hands up. "Dude. I'll let her read me the details."

"No, man. This is for you."

He held it out in his palm with the barrel pointing at the wall.

"I already have a weapon."

His eyebrows rose. What did he think? I wouldn't protect myself? "What you got?" he asked.

"It's a Smith and Wesson Shield .45." He didn't ask me how I got it, and I didn't offer the information.

"That's good for personal carry. This is a full-size Glock, carries seventeen nine-millimeter rounds. Take it." He offered the gun to me.

Holy shit. Seventeen rounds? I thought my gun was impressive with seven rounds. "Alright." I took it from him and inspected it. Nice looking gun. Not as heavy as I expected for a high-capacity handgun. He gave me four boxes of ammo. I locked them in the hidden safe next to the Shield. "You expecting vandals up here?" Maybe an all-out war?

"I have associates that would like to see this project fail. I promised you I'd keep your hands clean, but that doesn't mean I can protect you if they come looking to start trouble."

I nodded. I knew he had illegal ties when I took this gig. I could handle it.

"Can you shoot a gun?" Blythe asked.

"Of course."

"I can give you a lesson."

No way. Bad enough she'd be reading to me. Not taking shooting lessons from her. "Not necessary. You need me for anything else, cuz I'd like to get back to work?"

"That's it. I'm happy with the progress. Keep it up." Torrez patted me on the shoulder.

"Thank you."

Chapter 10

CECELIA

"What does a thesaurus eat for breakfast?" Zook broke the silence.

We'd been sitting at our usual tutoring spot in the library for about five minutes. Zook relaxed with his knees wide and his eyes watching me. I fumbled with my papers and snuck glances at his belt buckle, which was even more tempting today after what we'd shared Friday night.

"I don't know," I said without looking at him.

"A synonym roll."

I paused my preparation to watch his proud-of-himself grin.

The smile I cracked could not be held back, so I let the laughter flow through me. His smirk widened to a white-toothed smile. This is what Zook did to me, forced me to feel joy I'd denied myself for so long. I felt like Dorothy walking in the colorful part of Oz when I was with him. Too bad it was all temporary.

"No more distractions." I handed him a pen and today's worksheet.

"You are one giant synonym roll of a distraction."

"Do I need to get a ruler and smack your fingers?"

"No, ma'am, but I'd be happy to smack your ass if that's somethin' you'd enjoy."

Oh my.

And so we began this session as we had all our previous ones, with me blushing and embarrassed trying to focus on teaching and him laughing at me blushing and being embarrassed.

"Read these to me," I said in the firm voice I used when I stood in front of my students in the student teaching program.

"Th-rog?"

"Through. In this case *O-U-G-H* makes the *oo* sound. This one?"

"Roo?"

"Rough. In this case o-u-g-h makes the *F* sound."

"You're shitting me."

"No. *O-U-G-H* can make up to eight sounds."

"*O-U-G-H* can go pound sand."

"You'll just have to..."

"Memorize it. Got it. Why does English even have rules if everything is an exception?"

"Not everything is an exception, but there are many. Once you learn them though..."

"It'll be easy. Still waiting on the day any of this is easy."

"You're doing great. I'm proud of you."

I took a fortifying breath and peered into the azure blue of his eyes. The comfort they brought me would be gone soon. The glint of humor in them and the way he made me feel when he looked at me. Gone. Not mine.

"I've prepared these study packets for you."

"Okay..."

"They'll take you through third-grade reading and math."

"They will."

"Yes."

"And will you take me through third grade?"

"No."

He sat up and rested his elbows on his knees as his eyes narrowed in on me. "Are we back to this?" he said in a low whisper.

An uncomfortable itch bothered the back of my throat, but even coughing didn't clear it. "Yes. We need to end it."

He glanced out the library window. The weather had turned cold. Too chilly to discuss this outside. "Let's take this somewhere private."

"No."

"C'mon."

"I'd prefer to stay here."

"Come into the stacks with me." He angled his head to the tall shelves in the reference section.

I shook my head.

"Let's go."

When his fingers grasped my arm, I stayed put, keeping my head down.

He paused and sighed. His other hand slid up my back, leaving a trail of tingles on my spine. He wrapped his palm around my ponytail and gave it a firm tug. "Come into the stacks with me." His hand on my arm moved to my cheek and his voice lowered to a growl. "Now."

His commanding tone combined with the heat of his hands hypnotized me like the magician had done to the audience of his show. Zook could order me to plunge to my death at the end of the bluffs and I would obey. As I stood, the hand in my hair moved to my shoulder, guiding me deep into an old unoccupied section of the library.

He crowded me and the shelf shook when my back hit it. I peered up at him, feeling weak. His hands skimmed my hips and his thumbs dug into my ribs. "What's going on, CeCe?"

"I'm ending this." When he stood this close, the urge to kiss him overwhelmed me. He was too beautiful. Too flawlessly gorgeous.

"I get that's what you want. I need to know why. Are you spoken for?"

"What do you mean?"

"You belong to someone?"

"No." It was a half lie. Maksim controlled me like property, but I didn't belong to him. My heart belonged to Zook.

"Is it cuz I'm poor and stupid?"

"You're not. Don't say that. You're much smarter than me. You'll be a huge success."

His eyes scanned mine back and forth, searching for the truth, but I'd learned to mask it a long time ago.

"You don't want to be seen loving on a punk with a record?"

"No. Gosh. No." I hated the self-doubt I saw in his eyes. I'd never forgive myself for that.

"You're lyin'. This is all about your social status. Someone's forcing this on you and you hate it. Money doesn't factor when we're together and you know it."

"You're perfect. I was lucky to know you."

"Was? I don't get this. You didn't have any issues when you were coming all over my face a few days ago. You were all *yes, Zook, yes*."

He spoke the truth. Friday night I got swept away. I'd spent all weekend crying about today and what I had to do. "Please. Just let me go." I tried to pull away, but his strong hands forced my shoulders back against the shelves, his body pinning the rest of me. Pushing back on his chest did nothing to dislodge him. He had me caged. His spicy scent, the intensity of his tall frame, the passion in his eyes. My brain short circuited and I could barely form words. "I need to focus on my studies."

"No. You need me and whatever the hell I'm giving you that you aren't getting. You're scared shitless about what I make you feel. You've got some fucked up notion in your head that a woman should drop to her knees and serve. I'm challenging everything you think you know. And you're running from it."

"Please, Zook. Just... Don't fight this."

"Don't fight? Don't fight for you? For us?"

"Give me some space to—"

"Fuck space. I don't buy the drivel you're slinging right now."

"I— I'm sorry. Drivel?"

"Means nonsense. Bullshit. Which is what you're talking now."

My heart swelled with pride at Zook's expanded vocabulary. He'd come so far.

"You're scared. Let me tell you something about fear. I let fear rule my life, fear I'd lose my mom, my family. I lost them anyway. I hurt a woman. Probably screwed up any chances she had of recovering from some sick shit she was already suffering with. Went to prison, and I made a decision. I'm not letting fear rule me anymore. I got a second chance at life and I'm tackling it by the balls. I know there's better out there in this world for me and I'm fighting for it. I'll go down fighting for it. So you learn something from me, teacher. Don't do this. Fuck the fear and let me in!"

Tears rolled down my cheeks as a sob escaped my lips. I wanted to hug him and scream *yes*. He kissed me, and I kissed him back through my tears. A kiss goodbye. He wasn't buying my excuses about focusing on my studies, and he wouldn't let me get away with saying I was scared. I had to bring out the one thing that would really hurt him. He opened his mouth to deepen the kiss, his hips smashed against me and I groaned.

"Stop." My voice was weak. He nipped down my neck to the tops of my breasts. "Stop. It is my family. I can't be seen with an illiterate ex-con. They'll disown me. I'll have nothing."

His torso rocked back and he stilled. Pain passed through his eyes. Rejection he'd probably felt his entire life. Now I was using it against him. "You'd have me."

I shook my head. "Not good enough."

He wiped his lips with the back of his hand, the lust in his eyes turning black. "I see. Not sure if you're telling the truth or not. But I'm done.

I'm done trying to convince you we're right together. So fuck it." He snarled as he stepped back. "Go focus on your studies. Tell your family you dodged a bullet with a guy from the wrong side of the tracks. I got a damn house to finish. I'm so far behind schedule because of *you*." He jabbed a finger near my chest, but didn't touch me. "I don't have time to sit in the *Hale Library* getting my dick wanked around by some uptight *snob* lookin' down on me. I got money to make. I'll wager after I make it, like magic, once you see my fat wallet, you'll be crawling up my leg to get back on my dick. But don't be surprised if that spot's occupied. Plenty of women out there would be happy to have my *illiterate ex-con* cock in their cunt."

He turned and walked to the end of the aisle. His warmth left me and my stone heart crumbled to ashes.

Come back. Don't leave me.

He stopped at the end of the aisle and glared over his shoulder at me. "Goodbye, babe. Thanks for the fucking study guides."

My knees buckled and I slid to the floor, my legs bent in front of me. I hugged my knees and ducked my head. I couldn't watch to see if he took the study materials or not. It didn't matter. Why did I do that? Why did I say what I said?

Because I had to crush us. If Maksim found out, he'd torture and kill us both. I couldn't fathom the horrific pain Zook's death at Maksim's hand would cause. I'd seen him smother my beloved canary in his bare palms. I'd seen Maksim and his brothers rape and kill a girl before my eyes. Maksim was very capable of heinous things and he perpetrated them with no conscience or recourse. Doing this to Zook hurt, but putting Zook on Maksim's radar would be much worse.

No. The woman I was awaited me.

This alternate reality with Zook was a temporary fantasy. A cruel, ephemeral farce.

Chapter 11

NINETEEN DAYS AWAY from Zook. Not even three weeks since I'd seen him last and my world collapsed under the crippling pain. What was the point of all this without him?

Zook was a cool salve filling the divets of my scars, slowly curing my wounds. He gently wrapped bandages around my heart, and for a brief moment, I believed I could heal. Now I've ripped them off and rubbed salt in the open lesions, making it all so much worse than it was before I met him.

It wasn't his fault.

I did this to myself. I caused my own pain.

Why?

The logic escaped me in all the bitter tears.

I had to do it. To save him.

I need to save him. Right?

"Sissy, sit up. Time to eat." Soraya came into my room carrying a plate with a homemade Hot Pocket on it. She loved the stupid snack food, but I thought it was disgusting, so I taught her the recipe for a homemade version. We made it for each other as a simple gesture at our lowest times. It didn't help, but sometimes it was the only thing we could do. I'd made them for Zook, and he loved to tease me about my hot pocket. Sigh. I missed him and his jokes.

"Sit up. Take a bite. You haven't eaten since yesterday."

I pulled my torso up and leaned against the headboard. I'd been wearing the same T-shirt and yoga pants for days. I took the pastry and blew on it to cool it down.

"Professor Connery called my phone asking for you. He said you missed your office hours the last two days."

I nodded. "I know. I need to go. I've just lost track of time."

The bed dipped where she sat down. She placed a hand on my knee. "The first nor'easter of the season is rolling in tonight. Can't believe it's only the last Saturday in October. Isn't the first snowfall usually November or December here?"

"A storm?"

"Yeah, a big storm coming in. I stockpiled plenty of food and water. Got a generator in case the power goes out. I bought a Boston cream pie from Parker's for you. It's Boston Cream Pie Day. October twenty-third. We can eat it and watch a movie. What do you wanna watch? No romance. How about something scary?"

"You did all that? Not like you to plan ahead."

"I've been worried about you. All I can do is try to plan something. Anything."

"I don't know about a movie."

"You can't lie in bed crying anymore. You've made your decision and now we move on. We're strong. We can do this together."

"He hates me."

"I'm sure he doesn't. He's probably just confused."

I took a bite of the Hot Pocket, the gooey ham and cheese mixture warmed my cold soul. "He'll never forgive me for what I said."

"Go ask him."

"What?"

"Get out of bed, get dressed, drive up there, and say you're sorry."

God, I wish I could. "I can't. It's too risky."

"I'd take the risk, Sissy. If a man like Zook wanted me, I'd take the risk. I'm doing it with Cage. I haven't been caught."

"Yes, but you aren't me. And Yegor could catch you anytime. It's too reckless."

"Be reckless. Who cares? We're going to be miserable. It's inevitable. But like we always do, we enjoy our freedom when we have it. Then we have the memories to help us through when we go home."

She was right. Over the years, we'd allowed ourselves certain risks and pleasures. We'd actually gotten away with it too. Maksim and Yegor didn't check on us much anymore as long as we came home for Christmas and summer break. This semester was our last in the States before summer break. My last chance to have any pleasure. My last chance to be with Zook.

"Alright."

"Alright?"

"Yes. I'll do it." I climbed out of bed and headed to the shower. "Do you think I can make it up there before the storm?" The holes in my heart started to fill with the sweet hope of being with Zook again.

She beamed at me. "Yes, you could. It hasn't started snowing yet. They're still watching it off the coast."

"He was trying to get the roof done before the storm. I wonder if he did it."

"Go. Go see."

"Okay."

"And you never know what could happen. There's still eight months left before we have to go back. Maybe you and him can find a way to be together forever."

I turned and nailed her with a serious look. "No. No, Soraya. Don't push it. If I do this, it's temporary. We're not dragging him into this."

Her smile faded. "Whatever. Go now then. We'll worry about that later. This could be so wonderful."

Filled with Soraya's enthusiasm, I frantically showered, dressed, grabbed the Boston cream pie, and drove my Mercedes up to Province Bluffs.

ANXIETY BUBBLED IN my tummy like acid. This was impulsive and daring. Soraya was those things, not me. I tried to swallow the nervous energy as I drove, focusing on the possibilities. We could have eight more blissful months together. I need to convince him to forgive me and take me back. Then I'd have to lie to him. Inevitably, I'd have to crush both our souls. But it was too late to avoid pain. Might as well take what I could now, then hold the memories close as I nursed my broken heart back at home.

It felt like a race against the dark swirling clouds as I drove up the main road to Province Bluffs. The first drops of rain turned the fall leaves into a layer of rusted compost on the dirt road.

My breath caught in my throat when I reached the top of the drive. The house was stunning. It didn't have any siding or ornamentation, but the walls were up and it was grand! Several stories tall with round turrets at different elevations. A carved wooden door with a stained-glass window had been installed at the top of unpainted wooden stairs. Slate tiles covered the roof of the mansion, or most of it. He'd finished. I knew he would. Zook never failed. He was a winner.

His bike sat off to the side near his construction stockpile. Good, he was home.

I parked beside a shiny black Range Rover in front of the main entrance. It didn't seem like the kind of car Zook would buy. Perhaps he had a visitor.

A light rain tapped out drops on my hood and my cooling engine ticked in the silence. As I popped open my driver's side door, a threatening voice assaulted my ears.

"Don't move!"

All my muscles tensed. My fingers squeezed the keys, still in the ignition. If I'd been caught, I could start the car again and take off. I scanned the porch, fully expecting to see Maksim standing there.

I had to squint through the rain to make out the figure at the top of the stairs. A woman wearing a black pantsuit. Pointing a gun at my windshield!

"Stay in your car or I'll shoot!"

Oh my god. Panic zipped through my veins.

I'm going to die.

"Hands up."

I raised my hands through the open door.

"Who are you?"

"Cecelia." My voice shook.

"Speak up. I can't hear you."

"Cecelia," I said louder.

"Why're you here?"

"Is Zook here?"

"What the hell?" Zook burst out from behind her. "What's going on?"

"She says her name's Cecelia."

His hand pushed the gun barrel to the ground. "Put that down." He ran to my car. "Holy shit. CeCe."

Frigid rain peppered my face as he pulled me out and crushed my front to his chest. Cotton mixed with sawdust, paint, and manly sweat hit my nose.

"You're shaking like crazy."

"I- I'm- Zook..." I could barely speak.

"It's okay, baby. Shit. I'm so sorry." His arm around my back urged me toward the house, but the woman remained on the steps, her body tensed.

He pivoted so I couldn't see her. "Blythe, get the fuck out of here!"

She sauntered toward us with the gun pointed at the ground. Her hand still gripped it like she could raise it again if she needed to.

"Put that fucking gun away!"

"Sorry to scare your girlfriend, Zook." She didn't sound sorry at all as she tucked the gun into her purse. "See you next Saturday." She climbed into the Range Rover I'd parked next to. Her lights popped on and blinded me as she turned down the drive.

Zook tucked me in and kissed my forehead as she drove away. His lips were an elixir calming the shivers that had been racking my body. "She's gone. Come inside now. Let's get you out of the rain."

She's gone? Yes, but who was she? Zook had another woman at his place? A mean, beautiful woman wielding a gun to protect him? With the immediate risk gone, jealousy flooded my brain.

"I brought... pie." I pointed to the passenger seat of my car.

He leaned in and lifted out the box, grabbing my keys from the ignition as he straightened.

With one arm around my back and the other holding the pie and my keys, Zook guided me up the steps, through a huge foyer, and into the kitchen. He cleared some hammers, nails, and a drill from a countertop made of plywood and placed the box on top.

Our movements slowed and the house became shockingly quiet. The windows he'd installed muted the crash of waves on the bluff. The air in the house was chilly, but I felt a layer of sweat forming on my arms.

As I peeled off my jacket, I examined Zook. He looked deliciously sexy. Tiny drops clung to the beard covering his strong chin. His hair poked out in a floppy mess. Muddy brown clouds stained the armpits of his tee and the knees of his faded blue jeans. Off-white paint speckled the corded muscles of his arms. His eyes hung half-lidded and his shoulders hunched slightly forward as he crossed his arms over his chest and leaned back against the countertop. I was right. He'd been working to the bone to finish the roof before tonight's storm.

My skin heated as he perused my clothes. During a shopping trip to Barney's New York last month with Soraya, she'd talked me into buying these Yves St. Laurent black leather pants. She said they'd be fun to wear on Zook's bike, so I went for it. Tonight, I wore those pants with a dangerously low-cut Vera Wang blouse. Paired with matching leopard print belt and Louboutin ankle boots, the ensemble looked sexy and edgy. I figured if I wanted to earn his forgiveness, a fabulous outfit would help. By the way his mouth dropped open and his eyes darkened, I assumed he liked it.

He drew his gaze from my chest and plastered a frown on his face. "Why're you here, Cecelia?"

Oh shoot. Not the amiable welcome I was hoping for.

"I'm sorry," I said. "If you're busy."

"I'm not." Yep. Very angry. What did I expect after the way I'd treated him? I needed to break the ice.

"That woman— "

"Blythe?" His voice became even more gruff. Darn. I shouldn't have brought her up. "She works for my boss."

Okay. So a coworker. He hadn't mentioned her before. I thought he was working up here with a small crew of men. "She seemed very, uh, protective of you?"

"Yeah, shit. I'm sorry she scared you. I'll talk to her next time I see her."

Next time he sees her? "Saturday?"

"What?"

"She said she'll see you Saturday."

"Right."

I knew it. Zook replaced me without blinking. Here I'd been agonizing about being away from him, and he'd gotten cozy with some gun-toting woman in business suits.

"I- I should go."

"Why?"

"You had company. I interrupted whatever you two were doing."

"She was helping me read the plans."

So it wasn't a date? She helps him read the plans? "I could help you with that."

"I don't want you helping me with my work no more." I flinched at the harshness in his voice. He uncrossed his arms. "Why're you here, CeCe?" At least he'd gone from calling me Cecelia to calling me CeCe. A sign he was softening toward me.

"Well, uh, the first storm's moving in tonight. I assumed you'd be done with the roof. Thought you might like some pie to celebrate. It's Boston Cream Pie Day." God, it sounded stupid coming out of my mouth. "And you didn't call, so I uh, figured I'd come bring it to you."

"I didn't call."

I nodded slowly.

"*I* didn't call?"

"That's what I said."

"Last we talked, you said you wanted to end it because your family wouldn't approve of you with me."

"I did."

"And now you're rethinking things?"

"Yes."

"Why?"

Time to give him some honesty. As much as I could, I would give him. "I'm so sorry for what I said. You're right. I was... scared. I still am, but I never should've said such cruel things to you. But I can't stand it anymore. Being away from you is torture. I don't care what they think."

"You don't care anymore?"

"Nope. I'm taking a risk. If they disown me, at least I'll have you, like you said."

"Really."

I couldn't blame the skepticism in his response. He had no reason to trust me.

"Besides, I think you'll win them over with your charm and intelligence. Who could resist a gorgeous witty cowboy like you?"

His jaw worked as his eyes studied mine. He probably sensed I wasn't being completely honest, but all I could do was hope he accepted that.

"That is, if you still want me?"

Before I knew it, Zook's huge body covered me and pegged me against the kitchen wall. "I still want you. I'll never stop wanting you. Last three weeks, every nail I drive in, I'm wishing I was nailin' you. Every screw... I'm screwing you. Every time I'm hammering, well, you get the idea."

His mouth crashed on mine. Yes! My whole body ignited with the press of his lips. My fingers clutched at his shirt. I'd risk anything for this. I couldn't go another day without kissing Zook. I moaned into the kiss as his big hands came up and cradled my face in his palms. He ended the kiss and licked his lips. "What kind of pie did you bring again?"

His smile and easy mood caught me off guard. "Boston cream."

He chuckled. "Do they actually eat Boston cream pie in Boston?"

I loved how Zook forgave so quickly. It made me feel safe. With Maksim, even the smallest mistake would mean months of punishment and shame. With Zook, all was forgotten with one hot kiss. "I do. It's delicious. And we're not in Boston, technically."

"True. Let's eat pie then." He laughed and his weight left me as he turned to the kitchen counter.

"What's so funny?"

"I'm holding back my dirty jokes."

"Why?"

"You're too proper."

"I am not. I always laugh at your jokes, don't I?"

"You miss so many of my jokes, you don't even know I made them before I'm moving on to the next." He cut the pie and put a piece on a paper plate. He bowed as he offered it to me with a plastic spoon. "I'd very much like to give you a cream pie."

"Oh."

"See. You're a lobster and I just threw you in a boiling pot."

"Um..."

He smirked and watched me struggle. I'd missed his smile and his humor.

"God, you're hot as hell when you're turned on and embarrassed at the same time. My prim and proper tutor gets wet when I tease her."

"I do n—" I stopped myself because it was a lie. I totally get turned on by his jokes.

He grabbed his piece of pie and headed through an arched doorway leading to a sitting room with a high vaulted ceiling. "Come sit on the sofa with me. The fireplace ain't in yet, but I got some blankets and a space heater."

I folded my legs under me as we sat close together in the middle of a small loveseat. The view of the storm was awesome through the living room windows. Billowing angry gray clouds hung so low, they looked like a sponge dipping down to suck up the ocean.

"Wow. It's getting closer."

"Yep, I worked through the night the last three days. Got the roof done."

"I knew you'd make it in time."

"You always believe in me, CeCe."

"I do. I think you're amazing. I've told you that."

"It's my talented tongue. No woman can resist." He licked up the side of his pie slowly, scooping a dollop of chocolate onto his mouth. "Mmm. Shit, this is good."

"I don't mess around with pie."

He laughed again, probably thinking of more dirty puns.

"You make this?"

"No. This one is from Parker's. But I have a yummy version I make too. It has a layer of cheesecake. Tonight was kinda, uh, spur of the moment."

"It's fantastic. You'll have to make me yours someday."

"I'm glad you like it. And I will." I smiled and took a bite. The smooth chocolate ganache and vanilla custard blended with the sponge cake in an incredibly tasty combo.

"You ever had a Boston cream kiss?" he asked with a wicked grin and a tiny bit of custard at the corner of his lips.

"No."

He took a big bite and leaned in to kiss me. The sweet chocolate flooded my mouth. He moved slow, making sure I got a good taste of pie. And oh my goodness, the man could kiss! My body responded instantly. My heart rate picked up. My core tingled. After he'd licked every last grain of sugar from my lips, he pulled away and said, "Now you have."

Hmm? My eyes stayed closed and my tongue traced my lips. "Now I have what?" I asked dreamily.

"Had a Boston cream kiss."

"Yum."

We laughed as we ate more pie. All the tension from the drive here, getting a gun pointed at me, missing Zook for three weeks, disappeared when I was with him. He was optimistic and light-hearted and fun to be with. Not to mention so beautiful to look at. When I couldn't take another bite, I set my plate on the coffee table. He grabbed a blanket from the back of the couch, leaned back, and opened his arms and legs for me to climb inside. As his big warm arms surrounded me, a flash of lightning followed by the rumble of thunder rocked the house.

"Your work's gonna be tested soon," I said.

"Bring it on." His deep voice vibrated against the back of my neck.

"Is this house like others you've built?"

"In many ways, yes. Lots of rooms, secret passages. But this one has fancy shit. Rainfall showers and LED lights under the water. Why the hell would someone want their bath water to change color?"

"I don't know."

"I think some kinky bastard is gonna live here. There's so many shower heads, he's either planning an orgy or he likes his balls blasted with water."

"Secret passages?"

"Rich people have secrets." He nudged my ear with his nose. "They go out of their way to hide them. They trust me because they don't feel threatened by me."

"And should they? Trust you?" Should I trust you?

"If a man is honest with me, he can trust me. He screws me over, I know all his secrets, I won't hold back in using them against him."

"Like you did with Jeb Barebones?"

"Yep."

"What about your current boss? Torrez. Is he trustworthy?"

"So far, yes. I'm watching him close though. Not liking his right-hand man pulling a gun on you."

"Is that what he called Blythe?"

"Yeah."

"That's an odd way to phrase it."

He was quiet for a while. I flinched when lightning cracked. As the thunder rolled, he tightened his arms around me. "He offered to introduce me to his associates."

"Really? You know Boston's notorious for underground crime, right?"

"Yes. Heard all about it in prison. I wouldn't be surprised if Torrez was involved with the mafia. He said he'd keep my hands clean. Just wants me to build houses for him."

"I'm sure they say all kinds of things to grow their organizations."

"Shit. I'm sure they do. It doesn't matter anyway. I'm just using him to get started. I'm gonna be my own man. Not gonna answer to no one. I'm using Blythe too. Just so you know, I'm not attracted to her at all. She's too old for me, and the way she reads to me grates on my nerves."

I smiled with smug satisfaction. "Are you still going to let me tutor you?"

"Oh yeah. I'm learning so much from you. I'll always be grateful. When I walked out of prison a few months ago, never in a million years did I think I'd have a beautiful tutor and be living in a mansion I built myself. Things are going good for me for the first time in my life. Not gonna rock the boat now."

"Mmm."

"How about you, Cecelia Boujani? Are you happy?"

"Right now I am."

"What about before right now?"

I sighed. "I'm not sure."

"You're not sure if you've ever been happy?"

"It's a long story."

"I've got nothing but time. Where were you born?"

I knew this was coming. I'd mentioned my family, and now he had every right to ask me. "Atlanta, Georgia. We lived there till I was ten." I could tell him that much.

"And then?"

"My mom died." A lie. She became dead to me, but she didn't die.

"I'm sorry." The empathy in his voice jabbed into my conscience like a hot poker in a fire. I didn't deserve it.

"I went to live with my uncle." Another pseudo-lie. I was forced to live with a man who called himself my uncle.

"And where did he live?"

This was it. My chance to tell Zook the truth. *I was taken from the States, sold to a family in a foreign country, and forced to marry a man I barely knew*. But the truth would only give rise to more questions. *Will you be returning there after graduation*? No, it was best to lie. To keep the ugly truth from him so we could have this time together without worrying about the future or far off lands.

So while I burned to tell him, I kept the secret, saying the first city that came to mind. "Jacksonville, Florida."

His arms lifted me and turned me so I was facing him. I had to raise my legs over his thighs, opening my core to him. A swift heat filled the space between us. "Mmm. And were you happy there?" His voice sliced through me like hot velvet.

"Yes." His eyes watched my fingers fiddle with my pendant.

"You don't seem like a girl from Florida." Shoot. I should've picked another state. Why didn't I say Connecticut or Maine?

"There's all kinds of people in Florida. It's a big state." I also should've picked a state I knew more about apart from its size and the weather.

"What happened in Florida that caused all this fear in you?"

"Nothing." He wasn't going to let this go. All his attention was focused on me and getting me to tell him everything. The pressure welled in my chest. I wanted to tell him.

"I don't believe you."

"It's the truth." I closed my eyes because I couldn't stare into his intense gaze any longer.

"Are you close with your uncle in Florida?"

"No."

"But he pays for your schooling?"

"Yes."

"So he's just a pocketbook to you? But he must care about you if he wouldn't approve of me."

"Don't worry about him anymore, okay? When you meet him, he'll love you. Forget what I said."

"I'll drop it for now, but I have one more question."

I was sure he had a million questions. I wasn't giving him much to go on. "Yes?"

"Did someone hurt you?" He ran his hands up and down my back, gently trying to coax me to open up.

Yes. "No." I grabbed his head and desperately kissed him. *Please, Zook. Stop digging. I can't bear it. I'm your tutor and you're my student. Nothing else matters.* I climbed higher on his lap and ground my sex into his belly.

The sweet taste of sugar hit my buds when our tongues met. He kissed me with deep affection and longing. We needed to stop talking and kiss forever. His hands on my face pulled my head back, and he ended the kiss with a sigh.

"What's wrong?" I asked, breathless.

"I want you to tell me the truth now, before I fuck you." God, the authority in his voice was impossible to resist.

"We're not... I shouldn't."

"Oh, we're doing it. You could be gone again tomorrow, and I'm not letting you get away without being inside you like I been dreaming of since the second I saw you."

"The second you saw me?"

"Yeah. But don't change the subject. Tell me about your family. Your past. Why all this screwed up *I can't* shit?"

"I can't."

"Exactly." His hands lifted my hips and placed me back on the couch. He stood and strode to the other room.

Chapter 12

―――――

ZOOK RETURNED A SECOND later with a blue nylon rope wrapped around his knuckles.

"What's that?"

"Rope."

"And you need this now because?"

"I'm gonna break you." He snapped the rope taut between his hands.

"What?"

"When you get a skittish new filly, you gotta break 'em. They need to know you love 'em, but you're also the owner so what you say goes."

"Love? I'm not owned by anyone." That you know of. Why would he think he needed to own me?

"I'm not saying I'm your owner. I'm saying I'm gonna break you in so you trust me enough to let me guide you."

"With rope?" My voice hitched, and a tingle spread from my belly to between my legs.

"Yes. And Boston cream pie." He smirked and tilted his head toward the remaining pie on our plates.

"Oh." The tingle between my legs burst into full-on electric charges through my whole body.

"And a paintbrush." He held up an unused paintbrush with a wooden handle and long white hairs cut at an angle. A smaller brush, for detailed work.

Oh my. Zook wanted to tie me up and break me with pie and a paintbrush? I gulped down the lump in my throat.

"Don't worry, you'll love it. I will too. If you need me to stop, just say *Orion*."

"Orion?"

"My horse."

"You have a horse?"

"I did. Not sure where she is now. No changing the subject. Take off your blouse."

I could've said no. If I stood up and asked to leave, he'd let me. But lord help me, I didn't want to leave. Suddenly what he had planned sounded like the best idea in the world. Nothing else I'd rather do than have Zook tie me up with a blue rope and break me. I crossed my arms at the hem of my shirt and pulled it over my head, revealing a matching scarlet bra. As my hair settled, I peered up at him. His face had grown serious, and his eyes were dark. Within seconds, he was on me again, his mouth pressed to mine. His hand holding the paintbrush twined in my hair, and the hand holding the rope moved behind my back, caressing up and down my side.

"Love this bra. You look so damn beautiful. But gotta take it off." He unsnapped my bra and slid it down my arms. He planted his face in my cleavage and inhaled. "Smell so good, CeCe. Missed you. Missed your scent."

I grabbed his head and ran my hands through his hair, holding him close to my heart. "I missed you too, Zook. So much."

He took my hands from his hair and moved my arms behind my back. He kept his face in my chest as he twined the rope around my wrists and yanked it tight. As I gasped, he raised his head and gazed at me with a look so molten it could melt stone.

"Easy now. Trust me." He pressed on my shoulders till I was laying on my back on the couch. My tied hands pressed against my spine, and my head rested on the arm of the couch. "Atta girl." He unlaced my boots and tugged them off. He unbuttoned my pants and peeled them down slowly. The warmth from the space heater hit my skin. He kissed my belly as he lowered my panties and tossed them. I felt so naked, which I was, and he was fully dressed.

"Zook, please. Take your shirt off. Want to feel your skin."

He sat back on his knees, reached one hand back behind his neck and tugged off his work shirt. My goodness. Zook's body was so beautiful. All rugged cut lines, darkness and light, the flat plains of his pecs leading to the bumpy hills of his abs, and an ultra-masculine trail of hair from his belly button into his pants.

"Your pants too," I pleaded. If my hands were free, I wouldn't have to beg. I'd reach for his pants and rip them off.

"When I'm ready."

He gripped my ankle and lifted my leg up over the back of the couch. He placed my other foot on the floor, completely exposing my naked sex to him. "Stay like that. You look stunning." His voice reassured me as he picked up the plate of pie. He dipped the paintbrush in the rich yellow custard and smiled as he drew a stripe down my chest, from the dip in my neck to my navel. My nipples hardened at the cold, wet sensation down the center of my body. He looked at the trail of golden cream left behind and nodded, pleased with his work. He dipped his brush again and concentrated on my boobs like he was painting the Mona Lisa and each stroke had to be perfect. His brow furrowed as he worked from the swells to the tip, coating every inch of my breasts with Boston cream pie filling. The air tingled as the sweet cream dried on my skin.

I sucked in a quick breath as he scooted closer and his knee nudged between my legs. He tortured me as he formed precise peaks on my nipples. He moved down and painted chocolate ganache glaze around my sex. He chewed his lip as he swiped the brush from my opening up and over my clit. I threw my head back and it hit the arm of the couch. "God! God!"

He swiped the brush over my clit back and forth. A light touch, not enough to make me come, but enough to drive me crazy. "It's feels good, right? It looks fucking amazing. A masterpiece of sin."

"Please..." I wasn't even sure what I was begging for. I just needed him to move. I needed him inside me now. My knees shook with the need to wrap my legs around him.

Finally, he put the brush down. "Now I get to taste my creation." He licked from my belly button up between my breasts, up to my collar bone. His tongue swiped over his lips. "Yum. My god, woman, you're delicious."

"Please, more." My breasts jiggled as I struggled to get my hands free and the creamy peaks fell to the sides.

"Stop moving. You're ruining it."

"Argh!"

His mouth fell on one nipple, and I cried out as he sucked hard. He moaned around my nipple and the wetness, the vibration of his voice, it was all too much. I could almost come from that, even without him touching my clit. He licked the cream off my breasts by swirling his tongue in concentric circles outward from my nipple. He dove on the other nipple and sucked. This time he bit down, and a sharp pleasure mixed with pain shot to my core.

"Enough. Please. Take off your pants. I need you inside me. Please, Zook."

"Almost done. Just this last bit left." He ran his tongue down my belly and between my legs. His wet tongue licked all the chocolate around my opening. He groaned and pressed a flat palm to his dick through his jeans.

"I want to see your dick. Show it to me. Want to suck it. Taste it. Please."

"You're driving me insane, babe. Let me finish. This is the best part." His mouth finally landed on my clit. He sucked hard, lips and tongue devouring me like dessert. I cried out and lowered my legs. He quickly reacted and repositioned me open before him. He pushed two fingers inside me and the wetness gushed out onto his hand. "Soaking wet for me."

"Yes. So wet. Yes. Want you so bad."

His hot breath hit the skin of my navel. "You first. Remember. Always you first." He dove back onto my clit and kissed and licked. I squirmed under him. His hands held my hips down as he continued his torture. An orgasm I thought would crush me rose up from deep in my core and erupted out of me with a moan. An involuntary grunt escaped my throat as it pushed through me. As his tongue lapped at me, my body convulsed and shook.

My breasts heaved as I struggled to catch my breath.

Zook peered up at me with hooded eyes.

"Untie me now. Need to touch you." I rolled to my side and almost cried when his fingers worked the ropes loose. "Hurry."

As soon as my hands were free, they flew to his jeans. He'd already opened the fly so I pushed them down over his hips. He stood to throw them off with his briefs, and I fully saw him for the first time. His cock was just as gorgeous as the rest of him. I lowered my leg from the back of the couch.

I reached for him and he held me in his arms. Between kisses he asked, "Are you on birth control?"

"Yes."

"No condoms." His eyes were wild.

"Okay."

"I only want you. Nobody else. You're only with me, hear?"

"Yes."

"Atta girl."

Finally, he climbed on top of me and kissed me. The sugar exuded onto my tongue. I wrapped my legs around his back and pulled him close. He worked his tip into my very wet opening and nudged inside.

"So tight."

"More." I pushed harder with my feet at his back. His dick stretched my walls as he slid inside.

Deeper, deeper. We both grunted when his groin hit my clit and the tip of his dick nudged something inside me. "Damn, shit, fuck me. Fuck. So good. Wish I could last. Ain't gonna last."

"It's okay. It feels so good. Go ahead."

"You first," he said through clenched teeth.

"I already did. You're fine. Let go."

"Again." His hand reached down, and his thumb hit my clit as he started to move. He slid in and out and rubbed my clit in circles at the same time. The sticky mess between us grew warm from the heat of our bodies. His mouth fell on my breast again and when he bit down, it sent me sailing over the edge. His back stiffened and he groaned a long, tortured moan. We came together like that. Both of us gasping for breath, moaning, holding on tight.

A huge flash of lightning lit up the room followed by a loud rolling thunder, but it was nothing compared to the storm raging between us. Zook pumped into me a few more times, then started moving slower. He sucked my neck and kissed my earlobe. His short breaths caressed my ear.

We held each other and listened to the rain hit the roof as our heart rates returned to normal. He kissed my lips and my nose and turned my back to his front, snuggling his nose in my hair.

He didn't ask about my uncle anymore. We didn't talk at all. Everything had been said between us.

He was mine and I was his. Nothing else mattered.

Chapter 13

Cecelia

After a marathon study session, a glance at the clock told me I'd worked past midnight.

The big empty living room at Zook's place felt so lonely without him. Zook said he'd be late, but I didn't think he'd run this late. So here I sat on the couch, all alone in a big mansion on the bluffs.

My gaze stopped on the black and white picture I'd given to him for Christmas. Someone caught a shot of him wearing my sweater. The magician's eyes appreciated Zook's abs. Zook's mouth was turned down in a self-deprecating grimace. His eyes were on me and they were twinkling. I was laughing. I don't know if I'd ever seen a picture of myself smiling. I never let go and took risks. Only with Zook.

My eyes felt heavy. If I just took a quick nap on the couch, maybe he'd be back before I woke up.

ZOOK'S SOFT LIPS SKIMMED my cheek. My hands traced up the sinuous muscles of his back, my fingertips pressing into the taut muscle. Mmm. "You're back."

Through my blinking eyes, his outline came into view. He looked rough and scruffy.

"Yeah." My fingers trailed through the coarse strands of his hair. I liked it long like this. Easier to grab hold and tug. Which I did as I pulled his head down till his lips brushed mine. He chuckled and pulled back.

"Mmm. I was dreaming of you." My words came out sleepy and lazy.

"I know. I heard your sexy moans." His voice scratched like two granite rocks rubbing together.

"You were dancing and stripping out of a tuxedo."

I tugged his T-shirt up but it got stuck when he didn't raise his arms. "Don't tease me, Zook. Take off your shirt."

"Alright." He chuckled as he removed his tee. My fingers caressed down the smooth skin of his back and hit spikes on his belt. "You're wearing a different belt?"

"Not for long if this goes the way I'm hoping." Why did it sound like he was laughing at a joke I didn't hear?

His ass cheeks felt pert and round under the waistband of his jeans. "Commando?"

He pressed his erection into my thigh and trailed the tip of his nose down my throat. "Less clothes to take off."

God, the more he didn't kiss me, the more he drove me insane for him. I arched my back, trying to pull him closer.

"Damn, you're hot," he said, his voice strained.

"My hot pocket missed you."

"Did it now?" The steamy breath of his laugh tickled my neck, turbocharging my need for him. I kissed him hard and rough, biting his lower lip for taunting me. He groaned and finally, finally pressed his lips to mine. When our tongues met, he tasted different. Like cigarettes and beer, not his familiar toothpaste and Zook taste.

"Why do you— "

"Fucker!" Zook's voice echoed from the doorway. Zook's body flew off mine, and the room erupted into loud grunts and rustling. What the heck?

My heart raced as I fumbled for the light. Oh my goodness. It looked like two... two Zooks? Or two men who looked like Zook wrestling on the floor. One was wearing a black Bravo Construction tee and a cowboy hat, the other was shirtless, and oh my lord, blanketed in tattoos. But I swear, there were two Zooks fighting on the living room floor.

I scrambled to the far side of the couch to grab my phone.

"Don't call the cops!" Zook in the black tee stood up, holding his hand out to stop me. His hat had tumbled off and rolled toward the couch. Looking in his eyes, I knew. That was definitely my Zook.

"Why not?"

"'Cuz he's my brother."

His brother? What was his name again?

My body refused to move at first. What should I do?

His brother stood too and threw a vicious punch that crunched as it landed on Zook's jaw. Oh no. Instinctively, I ran to them and wedged my body between them.

Zook froze with his fist pulled back, his shocked eyes staring at me. "Get out of the way, CeCe."

"B-But..." Their resemblance stunned me speechless. His brother looked exactly like him but had longer, shaggier hair. His body was almost the same except for the tattoos. His brother's jeans hung lower on his hips and he seemed a bit thinner, but his shoulders were broad like Zook's.

Holy wowzers. The brother kissed me? And I didn't know it wasn't Zook? Both men had mad kissing skills. Now I was not the sort to entertain the idea of two men at once, but if it was two Zooks? Oh yeah, I'd be all over that. It was almost not like cheating. Almost. But not quite.

Zook pointed at his brother and gritted his teeth. "Don't touch my girl, Destry."

That's right. Destry. How could I forget such a unique name?

"Hey, man. She was begging. I had to assist." Destry's casual tone reminded me of the way Zook joked to get out of trouble.

"Like Lyric begged for you?" He spoke deliberately and pointedly, narrowing his gaze on Destry. Zook had never spoken to me like that. In all the fights we've had, he was never as spiteful to me as he was being to Destry right now.

Destry's brow furrowed and his body shook. He let out a feral growl and they charged at each other, but I put my hands up.

"Stop, you guys. Stop!" When my palm hit his brother's chest, the heat and steel of his muscles seared through me. All three of us stilled, our gazes traveling to my hand on Destry's chest. There, next to my pinky, on the solid plain above his brother's heart, was the same tattoo Zook had on his bicep. A bigger and sharper treble clef that looked like a curved dagger and five wavy lines of a music staff. Zook's music staff was blank and smooth. No notes. But Destry's tattoo had barbed-wire lines and letters stylized to look like notes scrolled over the staff. To-gether the letters formed the word "Lyric."

Who was Lyric? Whoever she was, Zook saying her name made Destry cringe and explode like Zook had rammed a hot poker in his eye. Zook wrapped his arm around my waist and pulled me up against his side.

"I did that for you," Destry said, referring back to the topic of Lyric. Oh my god. I was lost. What did Destry do to Lyric for Zook?

"Yeah, thanks for the favor, brother. It cost me two years behind bars." I'd never heard such bitterness from Zook before. He always accepted the time he served as his penance.

"You asked me to do it." Destry's growl sent a chill down my spine.

"That was before the FBI got involved." I felt Zook's arm get tight around me. He let go and stepped away from me like he was protecting me from his anger.

"Even after you got arrested, you still stuck to your stupid idea."

Zook smacked one fist into his palm and glared at Destry. "Yeah, well, that's me. The stupid brother, right?" He looked at the ground then raised one eye to level it on his brother.

"Shut the fuck up. Drop it already." Destry's shoulders got high and his voice raised.

Holy cow. They were going to fight again.

Zook shook his head. "No, I'm gonna bring it up and hold it over your head forever. Till you can't sleep at night."

"Fuck you." Destry gave Zook the middle finger with his curse.

Zook lunged forward and threw a punch, which Destry blocked, countering with a hit to Zook's chest.

"Stop! No more. Talk this out." I pressed a hand against each guy's shoulder, and they reluctantly let me pull them apart.

They glared at each other and huffed out harsh breaths. Destry's gaze shifted to my boobs in my tank top. I was breathing heavy too.

"Get your eyes off her tits, man." Zook's voice dropped deep and lethal.

"She's got beautiful tits, bro." Destry smirked at Zook and nodded toward me.

"I'll chop off your dick and stick it in a pickling jar. I'll throw your ass and the jar out the turret window. Did you know this place has a turret?" Zook cast a pointed finger at the ceiling in the direction of the spiral staircase. "Four flights up. I'll drop kick your pickled dick and your sorry ass out the fourth-story window. You'll both crash on the jagged rocks below. If you survive, you'll spend the rest of your life swimming around like a eunuch merman searching for your lost dick. Only to find out some octopus opened the jar and is wearing your dick as a necklace."

Destry stared silently at Zook for a moment then burst out laughing. "Really, Z? A pickled dick?"

I laughed too. I shouldn't because Zook seemed truly upset, but the image of the octopus wearing a pickled dick cracked me up.

Finally, Zook broke his stiff stance and chuckled too. "Seriously, Destry. This right here." He took my hand in his and held our joined hands over his heart. "This woman is all that I am and all that I have. Solely mine. Never cross the line."

My heart swelled for Zook. He'd told me and showed me he loved me with his gentle love, his fierce dedication, and all the little things he did. But this. This was huge. He'd placed our hands over his heart between him and his own twin brother. I'd never want to come between them, but I loved that Zook was making it clear to Destry what I meant to him. I nabbed my sweater from the chair. "Let's talk in the kitchen. I need coffee. And no more fighting like children."

"Fine." Destry grabbed his shirt from the floor and slipped on an old tattered tee that said "Snoop Doggystyle" and had a woman's naked rear end sticking out of a dog house. He looked around the place, his hair messed up and his face red from the scuffle. "Where's the kitchen?"

Good lord, both wearing black tees, you could hardly see any difference between them. I can't believe I didn't know Destry was his identical twin. This created a whole new layer of Zook for me to discover and love.

Zook waved toward the kitchen and Destry left us alone. "You okay?" Zook held my hand as he checked over my body.

"I'm fine. Nothing happened." Except I kissed him and asked him to take my hot pocket.

"Right. Destry's never at fault." Zook tugged on my hand. "C'mon, let me introduce you to my family."

Chapter 14

"CECELIA, THIS IS MY twin brother, Destry." Zook tilted his head toward Destry as we walked into the kitchen.

Destry closed the fridge, twisted open a beer bottle, and took a barstool at the island in the center of the room. He nodded at me with his lips quirked. "Pleasure."

My cheeks burned as I returned his smile. Destry was just as gorgeous and charming as Zook. "I'm going to make coffee." Coffee. Yes. Coffee would help me through all these confusing feelings.

"It's two in the morning," Zook said.

Oh. Hmm. "Decaf. I'll make decaf." Some kind of coffee was going to be made.

"What's with the hot pocket? She kinky like that?" Destry laughed and looked from me to Zook.

Oh my. I turned away and searched the cupboards for decaf. Did we even have decaf?

"How'd you find me?" Zook's angry voice hit my back.

"Vanity Barebones now Tessa Saxton," Destry answered casually.

"How'd you get in?" Zook had worked long and hard on the security in the house and prided himself on it.

"The alarm took a picture of my face and let me in."

Zook sat opposite Destry at the island. "Switching that damn thing to retina scanner tomorrow."

I found some decaf and got the machine started. The comforting sounds of brewing coffee filled the kitchen. Comfort was on its way. "Okay. Who is Lyric?"

"What does she know?" Destry asked Zook.

"A lot more after the fight we just had in front of her."

I grabbed a coffee mug and placed it next to my machine. "Who is Lyric and why did her begging cost you two years?" I focused on Zook because he was the one who should tell me.

They both kept their eyes glued to the countertop, looking like guilty puppies who had torn up the pillows while Mommy went shopping. "What did you not tell me? How did you sacrifice yourself for him? Oh my god! Is this about the rape conviction? Is Lyric the victim?"

Zook's head snapped up. His eyes begged me to stop asking questions. No way.

"Did Destry rape her, and you went to jail for him?"

Destry slammed his beer down and stood up. "I did not rape her."

"Then what the heck happened with Lyric? Tell me right now."

Zook ran his fingers through his hair and sighed. "Destry slept with her, pretending to be me."

"Did she know it was really Destry?"

Zook looked to Destry to answer. "I did everything I could to let her know it was me. Jeb was in the room. I'm not sure if she knew. We needed to convince Jeb it was Zook."

"This is crazy. Why would Jeb want Zook to sleep with Lyric?"

Zook stepped to me and placed his hands under my jaw, tilting my head up to look into his eyes. "I told you that part. Jeb declared me a seed bearer. He ordered me to sleep with Lyric. The part I didn't tell you was Destry had a history with her."

Destry turned his back on us, his shoulders hunched. I could see Destry's pain reflected on Zook's face.

"He'd been cast out. But I contacted him and told him the situation. He came back to the compound to help." Zook's voice held so much compassion. This wasn't easy for any of them. "I said I did it." His thumbs caressed my cheeks, his eyes warm and soft. Destry left the room, his head down.

"Why didn't you tell me?" He served time for a crime he didn't commit? And he didn't tell me?

"If anyone found out, Destry could be tried and serve time too."

"So you didn't trust me not to tell anyone, and you let me believe you raped that girl?"

"You loved me anyway. You believed in me and loved me despite it."

The coffee maker chimed my decaf was ready. His warm hands on my face made it incredibly difficult to think, much less stay mad at him. I broke out of his hold. "Yes, because I knew you were under pressure from Barebones. You paid your dues. But you could've trusted me with this."

He paced away from me and turned back to look at me. "What difference would it make? I was guilty. I didn't rape her, but I was guilty. I stood by while Jeb Barebones beat up Tessa. I did nothing when he pointed a gun at her head. I'm still guilty."

I took a deep breath as I poured my decaf into a Bravo Construction mug. "You were trying to collect evidence against him." I took my first sip and yes, yes, I could handle this.

"I did collect a shit ton of evidence, and I got a reduced sentence because of it. None of this matters. Our love isn't based on what we did or secrets we've kept. Our love is based on us. You and me. Here and now. Nothing could make me stop loving you."

He was right. Knowing this information about him didn't change the way I loved him. If anything, I loved him more because I knew him better. His arm around my shoulders pulled me close and he kissed me. I loved Zook and he loved me. Our secrets were irrelevant.

But... someone needed to step in and set these brothers straight, and now that I knew the truth, the responsibility fell on me. "Destry, come back in here."

He skulked back into the kitchen and sat down.

I started with Zook because I knew him best. "If you sacrificed yourself for him, you must love him. Right?"

"'Course I love him. He's my twin. He's in my head. I have to. Otherwise I'd be hating myself too. He's talented and smart. Unlike me. If one of us shoulda been free, it was him."

That was so Zook. Always wanting to give everything for the people he loved. I was lucky to be one of them.

I turned to Destry. "And you must be grateful to your brother for what he did for you?"

"I am." He leveled his gaze on Zook. "Thank you. Humbled by it."

"And did you make good use of your freedom?" I asked Destry.

"He did." Zook answered for Destry. "He took third place on Idol Factor two years ago. He just signed with Topside Records. He's gonna be huge." Zook beamed with pride.

"You follow me?" Destry asked with a shy grin.

"Absolutely. Took some grief in the slammer for spending rare TV viewing time watching myself on Idol Factor. Confused the hell outta them when they saw me up there singing those cheesy-ass songs."

"Dude. Those songs were so lame."

They both chuckled. I didn't know. I'd never followed that show, but I'd look him up as soon as I got the chance.

"Great. So you're a successful businessman, and he's a rising rock star, right?" I motioned from Zook to Destry.

"Right." They answered in unison.

"And you both did well for yourselves despite whatever happened years ago?"

"Right." Again, perfect synchronicity.

"So can we get past this and love each other? Because I've never had a brother before, and I'd love to know Destry."

Their eyes paused on me for a moment as they took in my words. Matching grins grew on their beautiful faces. Like it was choreographed, they bumped fists over the counter.

"Oh c'mon. It's been years. Go hug each other." I motioned with my arms that they should meet in the middle.

Slowly, they stood and walked around the island. They embraced and smacked each other's backs. The love radiating off them could heat this whole house in the dead of winter. Zook closed his eyes and tightened his arms around his brother. Destry rested his forehead on Zook's shoulder. Yes, they both needed that hug. Identical wounds were healing deep inside them. They broke apart and smiled at me.

Okay. Good. Next problem. "Now. If Lyric knew both of you, don't you think she'd like to know the truth?"

"We can't take that chance." Zook shook his head.

I understood how hard the truth could be to face, probably more than they did. "This poor woman. I think you should tell her what happened." Sure was easier to tell someone else to do it than to do it myself.

"We agreed we'd never tell Lyric." Zook's voice became louder and more stern.

"But..."

"No!" The anger in his tone made me flinch. "The issue is closed." I dropped my head and nodded like the subservient princess I was. The sharp edge of his tone hung in the silence. They had decided. For her. No one had asked Lyric. No. I needed to stand up for her now.

I locked determined eyes with Zook. "You need to contact Lyric."

"We keep her out of this." His voice softened. Admiration glowed in his eyes like it did every time I showed my brave side. And when he looked at me that way, I only felt more courage to speak up.

"You can't make that decision for her. She's probably going through hell, and you two have decided to keep the truth from her. Didn't you think of her?"

Destry leaned forward, his palms flat on the counter. "You think I don't think of her? I think of nothing else. If you believe for a second she's not in every song I write, every note I sing, you're mistaken."

Oh my god. Destry talked a lot like Zook. *Every nail I hammer.*

"Then why not go tell her?"

"It's like turning myself in to the cops." He took another sip of his beer.

"Not if she keeps the secret."

"She hates me. She'd love to watch the media shitstorm when this blew up."

"If she loves you like you love her, she will keep the secret."

"I don't love her."

"You do. Her name is tattooed over your heart. When Zook said her name, your eyes burned and we could all feel the pain pouring out of you. You said it yourself, she's in all the songs you sing. This isn't about her reporting you to the authorities. This is about the guilt you feel for leaving her for all this time. And if she did think it was you, imagine how confused she must've felt watching Zook confess and go to prison."

His eyes widened and he looked from me to Zook. "You had to go and pick a smart one. She's gonna walk all over us, Z."

Zook laughed. "CeCe can walk all over me anytime she likes. I'll lay down and let her do it."

"Yeah, me too." Destry wiggled his eyebrows.

"I'm tired," Zook said. "Let's go to bed."

"Where're we sleeping?" Destry asked.

"*We're* sleeping in our bed in the master suite." Zook took my hand. "There's ten empty rooms in this place. You can choose whichever one you like. Just stay the fuck away from CeCe."

"Deal."

"Goodnight, sucker. We'll see you in the morning."

"I'm a rock star. The morning is at least noon. Maybe later."

"CeCe has school all day. I have work. We'll meet you here for dinner tomorrow. I'll bring takeout."

"See you then, brother. Goodnight."

AS USUAL, I GOT HOME before Zook. I kicked off my heels and flopped face down in our bed.

Zook's warm lips touched my neck, and I twisted to my back to make sure it was him and not his hot rockstar brother.

"Hey, babe. Love having you in my bed when I get home from work." He kissed my lips.

"Love being in your bed." I smiled at him and he grinned back at me.

"I brought you moo shu from Takei Tommy's."

"Mmm. Yum."

"Where's the prodigal brother?" He looked toward the hallway.

"Don't know. Haven't seen him."

"Let's go eat." He wrapped an arm behind my back and helped me to my feet. "He doesn't show, more for you and me." He smoothed my hair over my ear with a sweet, loving look in his eye. Man, just being around him made me happy.

"Okay."

We walked to the kitchen. Zook grabbed some plates and the bag of food. "Let's sit on the patio by the fire. Grab a jacket. Sun's going down."

"Okay." The sandstone pit was built in to a table, so you could sit around it in a circle and eat. I snagged two beers, a bottle of chardonnay, and a glass for me. I slipped on my jacket and a pair of shoes I kept by the door. Zook and I loved to cuddle and chat by the fire.

The flames flared to life as I spooned the food onto our plates. Destry appeared in the open sliding door and rested his shoulder against the door jamb as he yawned. "Mornin'." His voice scratched as he scrubbed his hand over his face. He still wore the same jeans and tee as last night, but he'd added a black leather jacket with bullets draped over one shoulder. He was a grungy replica of Zook.

"You're just getting up?" Zook asked him. "We worked an honest day already."

"Telling you. Vampire. Sleep all day. Wake at night." He squinted into the evening sun as he took a few steps outside. He eyed the Chinese food cartons on the table surrounding the fire pit.

"Sit down and eat breakfast then." Zook pushed a plate in front of an empty seat close to Destry.

"Don't mind if I do." He sat down and accepted a beer I offered him.

As we scarfed down moo shu pork in little Chinese burritos and spicy kung pao chicken, I noticed something new. The restlessness in Zook's hands had left. He chewed with a relaxed jaw. Comfort flowed between them like a part of him had returned and he was whole again.

Zook peered at Destry over the fire. "So why'd you come besides you want to connect with me?"

"Isn't that enough? Family is forever." Destry leaned back in his chair and spread his knees. Curly dark hair and the white cotton corner of his pocket showed through the shredded holes in his thigh.

"Not our family. Why'd you come to Boston?"

"Mom needs our help."

Zook dropped his fork and stopped chewing. "Mom? You know where she is?"

"She's in Idaho."

"With Dad?"

"No. Dad left her. She's married to Elder Grimsol now."

Zook grimaced. "God, how old is he?"

"Ancient."

"Tell me what you know."

"They're poor. Jeb's losing control and out of money. She's ready to leave, but scared. Doesn't know how. Begged our forgiveness and help."

"Huh." Zook scratched his chin and looked to me.

"Wait. This is the woman who let Jeb force you to work since you were children? The one who didn't teach either of you to read? Didn't fight for you? And now she wants you to help her?" Anger bubbled up in my throat, but I bit my tongue because she was still their mother. "Can you forgive her?" I asked Zook. She caused so much misery and now Jeb is in prison and she's out of money, she wants her sons, who became successful despite her, to bail her out?

"If she's willing to leave the cult, I'm willing to forgive her. We all did things we regret under Jeb's command. I've been granted forgiveness by those I hurt, she deserves it too," Zook said.

"And you, Destry? Didn't she disown you when you were cast out? Can you forgive her?"

Destry nodded, his face grim. "I can. But I'm not going back there. I won't go see her while she's inside. That's why I needed Zook."

"I'm not going back either." Zook's voice had a finality to it as he resumed eating.

As we finished our food, Destry remained quiet and stared at the fire. Zook asked me about my day and we talked briefly. But the topic of his mom hung heavy in the air, all of us contemplating how to handle this new information.

Zook leaned back in his chair and gazed out at the sunset. A layer of yellow and orange faded to deep blue at the top. "I'll write her a letter."

Destry sat up straight and raised an eyebrow at Zook. "You're going to write a letter?"

Zook nodded. "Cecelia taught me to read and write." He smiled at me and grasped my hand. "This will be good for me. I'll write her a letter telling her we love her and we'll help her if she agrees to leave the Brotherhood behind. No more Jeb or talk of damnation. If she's willing to accept us as we are, she can be part of our lives. We'll pay for her to relocate and we'll support her financially and emotionally. Agreed?"

"Sounds good to me." Destry downed the last of his beer. "I knew you'd fix this for me."

"Let's wait and see if she agrees. She might want our money but not be willing to give up Jeb. If that's the case, no deal." Zook packed up the empty cartons and tossed them in the trash. He walked to the kitchen and came back with two more beers. He handed one to Destry and topped off my wine. "I'll write to Mom tomorrow. Tonight, I'm catching up with my twin brother and spending time with my girl."

He pulled me into his lap and Destry smiled. This was nice. I liked having Zook and Destry together. It felt right and I was happy Zook had part of his family back.

Chapter 15

THREE MONTHS LATER

Zook

I walked down the Hale corridor like I belonged here.

When you appear confident, people don't question you. In the nine months I'd been dating CeCe, I'd been to her office once. Her professor was there, so I made up some shit about class work, and he bought it.

Hopefully, the prof wasn't there today. With the house almost done, and my stress level down, I could focus more attention on her. CeCe had final exams and spent all day in her office. One thing I knew how to do, calm my girl down when she felt stressed.

I held a cup from the Golden Goose Bistro in the doorway, jiggling it like a puppet.

"Hello, teacher. Can you spell caffeine?"

She laughed.

"Spell caffeine correctly, and you'll win this magical coffee made by golden geese."

"*C-A-F-F-E-I-N-E.*"

"Ding, ding, ding. You are correct!" I had no idea if she'd spelled it right, but I figured she did. I walked in her office and set the cup down next to a stack of papers. She grabbed the cup and inhaled it.

"Thank you, thank you, thank you." She swiped at a hair in her face. Her eyes were wild, like she needed that coffee to live.

"You're way too stressed." I placed my palms flat on the desk and gave her a smile. That usually helped when she was anxious.

She shook her head and rattled the papers. "I have to grade all these exams for Professor Connery *and* finish my thesis by Friday."

"You need to take a break."

"A break? No. I don't take breaks. I just go go go. Breaks are for weaklings."

"Breaks are for sanity." When I stood behind her chair and bent to kiss her neck, she stiffened. "You need to unwind."

She sighed and angled her head. "Professor Connery could come in anytime."

I nibbled up to her ear. "Mmm. That would be hot."

My lips moved from her ear to her mouth. The taste of coffee and her warm mouth made me moan. I peppered kisses from her collarbone to her cleavage. "You taste good upside down."

"Really, Zook." She was breathless. "I could get in so much trouble. There's only two weeks left."

"Mmm." I rolled her chair out and kissed over her blouse to her belly button. "Okay. I'll leave your clothes on. Just in case."

Moving to my knees in front of her, I slid up her skirt and kissed up her gorgeous thigh. She sighed and groaned but didn't stop me. Pressing her legs wide, her scent hit me. CeCe's unique smell always made me want to come in my pants.

"Heaven right here between your legs."

She wiggled her hips to help me get her skirt high enough so I could get to what I needed.

"Damn, so beautiful. It's all one hundred percent perfect woman right here." I kissed her mound through her underwear. Navy silk today to match her skirt.

She squeaked and her hips surged up.

"Come here, girl." With my hands on her hips, I tugged her forward. If anyone walked in, they'd think she was slouching in her seat, which she never does. My girl has rod-straight posture.

I slid the crotch of her panties to the side and dove in for a kiss. She was already wet for me. "I can see you're relaxing."

She laughed and sucked in a huge sharp breath when I licked her slit from bottom to clit. "So good. So damn good, CeCe. Every time." I slid two fingers inside her hot wet cunt and teased her G-spot while licking her clit.

"Oh!" Something slapped the desk, presumably her hands.

I chuckled. She was totally losing it up there. Hell, I was losing it down here. I unbuttoned my jeans and palmed my dick.

Her thighs clenched and her knees closed around my head. Was she coming already? That's my girl.

"Hey, can you talk?"

Huh? She wanted to talk? No, wait. Not her voice. Someone had entered her office.

"Um, can it wait?"

Oh shit. CeCe had a visitor. Sounded like her roommate, but I couldn't be sure. Either way, I had to get CeCe off quick so she could talk. I pushed her knees against the insides of the desk and drilled my tongue in, sucking hard.

"Oh. Oh. Ahh..." Her hips flinched and shook.

"Are you okay? You seem out of breath," her friend asked.

"No. I'm uh, fine. Just surprised to see you here."

I loved listening to her stumble. Her short breaths told me she was close. Normally I'd tease her, but since we were in a clinch, steady firm pressure would get her off fastest.

"I need to talk to you." Her friend started talking. Good, give CeCe some time to come on my face.

Finally, CeCe gasped and pulsed on my lips. Her legs closed around my head as I lapped up every last drop from her, dragging out her orgasm as long as possible. I squeezed the base of my dick. I had to wait. Couldn't jack off under her desk without being heard.

CeCe's muscles relaxed and I caressed her knee.

"What's going on, Soraya?"

Ahh, yes. Her roomie. Not so bad if we got caught.

"I'm thinking I made a mistake with Cage." Soraya's words dropped off at the end, like she was holding back tears.

"What's wrong?" Cecelia forced her skirt down as she stood up. "Why're you wearing sunglasses in here?"

"It's just bright," Soraya responded.

"Bullpuckey. Take them off." Cecelia walked out from behind the desk and sucked in a quick breath. "Oh my gosh. What happened to your eye?" The alarm in her voice snapped me out of my haze. "Your cheek is swelling."

"Nothing." Soraya's voice broke and cracked.

"Did Cage do this?"

"He lost his temper." She spoke quietly.

Holy shit. He hit her? I knew Cage. I'd seen him at their apartment. Jarhead. He seemed like an okay guy to me. A little distant, but never thought he'd hurt Soraya. My throat tightened, and I dug my nails into my jeans to hold back the shit I wanted to start screaming.

"Oh my god, Soraya." Cecelia's voice was deep and scratchy.

"I pushed him. Asked him about marriage again. I shouldn't have, but there's only two weeks to graduation. I blew it. I screwed up the whole plan. If I'd waited till it was time to leave, he probably would've asked me. But I was getting nervous. So I pushed it. He flipped out. Said I was a golddigger. Trying to trap him."

Cage would pay for this. He would fucking pay.

"I told you this wasn't the way." Cecelia's voice muffled like she was hugging Soraya.

I rose to one knee, preparing to stand up and talk to Soraya when she said, "Zook's your last chance."

I froze.

They were quiet for a long time.

Zook's your last chance?

I'm her last chance? Chance at what?

What the fuck?

"No. Don't bring Zook into this."

"He's your ticket, Cecelia. You have to get him to marry you."

Holy hell. Her ticket? My heart stopped beating in my chest, and I swear I could hear Cecelia's pounding on the other side of the desk.

"Shh. Stop. You're upset. Let's get out of my office."

No. Let's stay here, Cecelia. Why am I your ticket? Your ticket to where? I'd love to hear all about it. In the last six months, she'd given me bits and pieces about her life. She told me she'd dated a guy named Max, and it wasn't a healthy relationship. That's as far as we'd gotten with her trusting me.

Soraya sniffled, and I heard the tear of a tissue from a box. "This is such a mess. Marry Zook. Stay here in America."

Stay in America? Was she leaving?

"Get away from Maksim once and for all."

Maksim. Max.

The name hit me like a sledgehammer.

"God, Soraya. Please be quiet."

"Did you tell him?" Soraya whispered.

"No." Her voice was sad, broken.

Just like my heart hiding under the desk, dying inside listening to every damn word of her fucking secret. No, she didn't tell me anything.

"Zook will take care of you. Go for it. Please. At least one of us should."

My back hit the desk with a thump.

"What was that noise?" Soraya asked.

"Uh, nothing. I just remembered I'm supposed to meet Zook at the bistro. Let's go."

Another lie.

"Ask him about marriage. He won't hit you. He loves you."

No. I won't hit her. I was planning to ask her to marry me. Before this. Before I knew... What did I know? Nothing. Nothing except I had no idea who Cecelia Boujani was. I had no proof she really loved me. No way to know she wasn't using me as a *ticket*. A ticket to stay in America.

"No. Not that way. He's not the answer."

The answer to the question she never asked and never will.

"Let's go get you some ice."

Their feet shuffled toward the door.

"Wait in the hall for me. I need to get my purse. I'll take care of you. Don't worry."

"I love you, Sissy. You're all I have."

"I love you too, Soraya. We'll get through this. Together."

Yes, those two together in their charade. Cecelia and I apart. Over.

Her heels appeared before me. As she bent to remove her purse from the drawer, she peered down at me. I could barely look at her.

Guilt. All over her face, dripping from her eyes.

"I'm sorry. I didn't want you to find out this way," she whispered.

I didn't reply. If I hadn't overheard her conversation with Soraya, she would've never told me. After all I'd done to earn her trust, she couldn't tell me the truth.

"We should call the cops," I said.

Her eyes widened. "We can't. Please don't call the police."

"Why not? Cage needs to pay for this."

"We'll talk later. Just please don't call anyone."

"Go see to her," I said.

She grabbed her purse and ducked out with her head low.

Climbing to my feet, my head thumped against the desk. "Shit!"

What the hell just happened? Whatever it was would have to wait. I needed to pay Cage a visit first.

Chapter 16

THREE HOURS LATER, I parked my bike in front of her apartment and rang the bell. My fingers throbbed and my knuckles ached. My jaw pulsed where he'd gotten a few in. Big motherfucker. Using his strength against a woman...

Smashing Cage to a bloody pulp didn't calm my anger. The adrenaline in my veins could pilot a jet plane across the Atlantic. I should go back and beat his ass again.

Nothing would change the fact Cecelia had been lying to me. Why? That one question repeated in my head more than any of the other bazillion questions I had.

She opened the door slowly. Tight leggings, an oversized sweatshirt, no makeup, hair tied in a loose ponytail, eyes red and puffy.

God, she looked exquisite.

My fingers itched to pull her in my arms and kiss her till she screamed in ecstasy. But instead I said, "Hey."

She stepped back and motioned for me to come in. Her eyes stayed focused on the floor as I walked past her. "Hey."

The guilt in her voice socked me in the gut harder than anything Cage could dish out. Sometime in the middle of teaching Cage the lesson of his life, I'd convinced myself it didn't happen. I must've misunderstood the conversation in her office. The shock made Soraya talk nonsense. It couldn't be true.

Because my girl loved me and I loved her. No way she kept life-changing secrets from me at the same time she bared her soul to me. But the defeated way she said *hey* made the sand of betrayal pummel my head again.

"Soraya okay?" I asked her.

She closed the door and nodded. "She's resting."

"Cage won't be a problem anymore."

Her head snapped up, and she met my gaze for the first time. Her eyes scanned my hands and face, bloody evidence all over me.

"Thank you. You don't owe us anything."

Oh really?

I rushed her, and my torso smashed her to the door. She gasped and turned her head to the side. With my lips close to her ear, I asked, "I don't? I'm not obligated to protect you?"

"No." She whimpered.

I had to know. How far back did her lies go?

"Tell me something, princess. Who pays for your schooling? Your Mercedes? Your fancy clothes?"

"My uncle."

"Is his name Maksim?"

"No."

Fuck. This was so confusing.

"Are you leaving the country?"

"Yes. After graduation."

"Where're you going?"

"I can't tell you."

"What's your uncle's name?"

"I can't tell you that either."

"Why're you here going to Hale?"

"My uncle sent me to America for my schooling. Please stop asking these questions."

"Stop asking? Stop asking questions about why you lied to me for nine months? Nine months I fell in love with you? The whole time thinking you were mine?"

She shook her head.

"We were living the dream, babe. You were it for me, and I was it for you. I knew you had issues with your family you weren't willing to share with me, but this? Fucking blindsided by this."

"I'm sorry."

"Oh, you are? Does that change anything? You had no plans to tell me you're returning to this unnamed country after graduation?"

"No."

"Fuck! Who is Maksim?"

She flinched and looked to the floor. She didn't need to answer. The drop of her shoulders told me he was the one who had taught her to kneel and perform oral sex like a slave.

Rage seethed through me. "You won't tell me? Show me." My hand wrapped around her neck. "On your knees. Show me who Maksim is."

Her eyes widened and her mouth dropped open. I took that as my invitation to shove my tongue in there. Damn CeCe. She kissed me back, and our tongues battled. CeCe's kisses were always desperate. Now I knew why. She was thinking of him.

I tore my lips from hers. "On your knees."

And damn, damn, damn. She did it. She got down on her knees, head down.

"Open my belt." She hesitated a split second. I'd never forced her to do anything before, and I'd never allowed her to kneel before me. I always let her climb me and find her way to what she wanted. Always gently guided her, trying to avoid exactly this situation.

And I hated it, but seeing her like this made me hard. I bet Maksim liked it too.

"Suck my dick like you suck his."

She whimpered, and the windows to her soul closed in her eyes. She opened my belt, lowered my briefs, and pulled out my hard cock. She wrapped her lips around my head and... fuck me. It was pathetic. Nothing like the times she was on top of me, suctioning my dick. It lacked passion. It was automatic. She performed her duty.

"I asked you if you were spoken for and you said no. Did you lie then too?"

She shook her head no as much as she could while keeping my dick in her mouth.

Bullshit. She belonged to Maksim.

"I fell hard for you. I wanted to marry you. Was I your ticket out? You want to move on from Maksim to me? Your next meal ticket?"

She kept bobbing her head, performing her half-hearted blowjob like she wasn't ripping us apart.

"Tell me the truth now. Last chance, babe. Last fucking chance and I'm gone. Your meal ticket walking out the door."

The first tear dropped down her cheek.

Enough. I'd had fucking enough.

With my thumbs behind her ears, I pulled her head off my dick. "I don't believe it. Not one second. I may be stupid, but I don't believe you were after my money."

"No. I loved you when you had nothing." More tears fell to the carpet. "I haven't slept with him in six years."

What the hell? "What power does he have over you? Tell me and I will fix this."

"No. Please. It's not that simple."

"Explain it to me then. Spell it out for the imbecile who can't read and can't make heads nor tails of your bullshit right now. Do you regret us?"

She pressed her lips together and finally whispered, resigned. "I'm going back. To protect you."

To protect me? From him? Didn't she believe in me enough to keep her safe, no matter how powerful Maksim was?

"I would fight for you." I pushed my bloody hands into her hair. "I'd kill for you. I'd go back to prison for you."

She whimpered.

"I'll kill him. I'll kill him for doing this to you. To us. Tell me who he is and I'll kill him."

Dropping to my knees, I gripped her head, harder than I should. "Marry me and stay here with me. I'll give you everything. I'll protect you with my life."

"No." Deadpan. Lost. My Cecelia was gone. I didn't recognize the girl on her knees in front of me. A vacant hotel room.

I kissed her. Smashing my mouth to hers. *Come back, baby*.

She didn't kiss me. Her lips were as dead as her soul. I pulled back and stared into the void of her eyes. "Say yes."

"No." Still dead. Lifeless. Hiding.

I had to bring her back. The only way I knew how. I kissed her. It was like kissing a corpse, but I pressed on. I couldn't give up on her. I couldn't lose her like this.

Finally, with a whimper, life flowed from her again. She kissed me back, and we kept at it until we panted for it and fire blared between us.

After endless minutes of hot and heavy kissing and touching and grasping, my CeCe returned. She squeezed my cock like she always did. Aggressive, assertive, my girl.

I ripped her pants off and moved over her, guiding my cock and entering her. We both groaned. She couldn't deny this.

"Did you ever love me?" I said with my lips by her ear, my thrusts slow.

"Yes. I loved you. I love you. It was real." She cried against my lips as she came, the pulsing forcing me over the edge too. And for a moment, the world consisted of us alone. Nothing but our bodies and pure overwhelming bliss.

But all too soon, it passed, and our breathing evened out. Tears covered her face. Blood coated my hands. Her wetness engulfed my cock.

With a final press of my lips to hers, she left me. She closed her eyes, and the walls came up.

I pulled out and rested my forehead on her chest. "Tell me who he is, and I will do whatever it takes so we can be together."

She shook her head. "I'm so sorry."

I stood and she stayed on the floor, refusing to open her eyes as I buckled my pants. "I've learned one thing in my life. Don't allow fear to choose your future. Fight for your destiny even if you're afraid."

Again, she shook her head, charring my soul with her tears.

"There's no solution here if you don't stand up for yourself and for us. If you choose to return to this Maksim asshole, it's over. We're over. All we had is erased. Like a misspelled word. Erased. The dust swept to the floor and forgotten."

She covered her face with her hands and wept. Lying half-naked on her floor. She wept, but she didn't stand up and fight for us.

"Once again the student is smarter than the teacher. You know how many people out there dream of a love like ours? I've seen men rotting alone in jail with nobody to love them. Women stuck in marriages with men they didn't love. We had something true and free. And you're tossing it to the curb like spoiled food. Well, go ahead. Make that decision. I'll honor it. But when you're in your secret country, with Maksim, remember tonight and what pure love feels like. And know we had everything, and you threw it away."

I left her lying like that, closing the door and leaving the ashes of my heart behind me.

TWO LONG WEEKS WITHOUT Cecelia. Knowing she was at home or at school and I could still reach her, but couldn't call. It broke me.

The last two weeks we could've spent together, wasted like trash. We could've been making love, milking every last drop out of it. Instead we were deep into the pain of losing each other. Neither one of us willing to break down and give in. Destry tried to convince me to go to her, but my stubborn pride stopped me every time.

"Cecelia Boujani, master in education, magna cum laude."

She walked up to the stage at her commencement ceremony. She'd earned her degree. An accomplishment she'd worked hard for and deserved. God, she looked stunning. Her chestnut hair shined in curls down her back. Hair I'd caressed every night as she fell asleep. She made the square hat on her head look like a tiara and the table runner look like a Miss America sash. Cecelia could wear anything and look like a million bucks.

I stood beyond the fenced-in area designated for the graduation ceremony. An outsider peering in. A cowboy in a sea of socialites.

As she stepped down the stairs, our eyes caught. I removed my hat so she could see the hurt on my face. The love I felt for her stained by her lies.

She raised a hand to wave.

I lowered my gaze and turned my back on her. "Fuck."

I'd watched her graduate. The end. No more chances for me to change my mind and chase her. No more time for her to run to me and make this right. We would end like this. She'd take her secret with her home to wherever she was from. I glanced over my shoulder. The tears streaming down her cheeks cut like a dagger.

But you got what you wanted, babe. You used me when it was convenient and discarded me when you were done. Have a nice flight back home.

I strode out of the Hale campus for the last time.

Chapter 17

———

ZOOK

My heavy steps sprayed gravel from under my boots.

Blasting wind and a blaring horn caused me to raise my head and wake the fuck up.

Shit. I'd drifted into the road. Almost got myself killed.

Sloping over to the shoulder, I trudged up the hill to the Bluffs. Never knew this road was so damn steep. Where the hell did I leave my bike anyway?

Oh that's right, at the pub in town. Too drunk to ride. Last thing I needed was a DUI added to the list of ways I was fucked.

I shouldn't have drank so much. Emptying all the whiskey bottles in that joint didn't dull the edge of the piercing pain. Two weeks ago, Cecelia carved my soul up like a pumpkin. Today, the rotten carcass finally caved in.

She left hours ago.

Right after graduation, Cecelia took a taxi to JFK Airport... Yes, I followed her. Two men escorted her onto a Turkish Airlines plane to Moscow.

Even if I had a ticket I couldn't go after her. I'm on parole. I can't travel out of the country.

The rock I kicked tripped along the road in front of me.

No song I could sing would make her come back. No joke could make this funny.

CeCe left her mark on my heart. I'd never met a woman as gorgeous and smart as her. She lit up when I kissed her. She laughed at all my jokes. She never made me feel stupid for all the words I couldn't read. She made me feel like I could climb mountains if she would just laugh for me. I'd fallen in love with her body, every curve so smooth and appealing, like a whittled piece of oak, you can't help but run your fingers over the grooves.

But now my hands that were always working, always touching, hung useless at my sides. I could create nothing.

The wind whispered *failure, failure*. Unworthy of heaven, a rapist, a Son of Perdition. Nowhere to go but hell.

The screech of a siren stopped me in my tracks. Oh shit. The cops! I scrambled down the embankment and hunkered behind a tree.

The whirring noise came closer and red lights flashed up the deserted road.

Not cops. A fire truck.

The sound zoomed past me. Some rich bastard up the hill probably had a heart attack while fucking his mistress.

Two more trucks zipped by as I passed the last lot before mine. The last lot before... mine?

Fire trucks were going to my fucking mansion?

No!

My boots skidded in the dirt as I took off running up the hill. I smelled the acrid smoke first. Rounding the corner, a huge black cloud came into view.

Flames engulfed the back half of the house.

One truck sprayed three thick streams of water from an extended ladder over the house. Several men on the ground held hoses aimed at the crackling flames.

"Fuck!"

All my work! Burning to the ground. I could hear it. Cracks and pops of my efforts, disintegrating.

Cecelia! Need to save her. No. No, she's not here.

Destry had rehearsals tonight.

I didn't own anything valuable. Did I? I'd put Tessa's journal in the fireproof safe but one thing...

Oh shit! I need to save it!

I raced up the steps and pushed through the front door.

"Hey! Stop!" someone yelled at me, but I'd already made it to my room in the back.

The flames licked up the hallway and water crashed on my head. I dove for my nightstand.

Got it! The box containing Cecelia's ring.

"Get out of here, now!" The fireman who followed me in yanked my arm back.

I swiped the framed picture of us from the mantel and coughed as I ran back out.

"Stay here. Let us do our job."

"Yes, sir."

He was pissed, but I had her ring and the picture she gave me.

Everything else could burn.

———

AN HOUR LATER, I SAT with my ass in the dirt that would've been a tennis court. The saved picture of our date to the magic show lay next to me. The ring in my pocket.

Torrez' shoes tapped out steps toward me. "Guthrie, you alright?"

"I'm sorry, man." I ran both hands through my hair and pulled as another cough burned from my lungs.

"For what?"

"I blew it. Burned the place down."

"You burned it down?" He didn't seem upset considering his house just went up in flames.

"Must've been somethin' I did. Electrical, space heater, I don't know. You're gonna fire me today. I didn't finish in time."

"What in the sam-hell nonsense are you spouting at me?"

"I failed. It's over. Deadline was today and you don't have a house. No fuckups. No excuses. She's gone. The house is gone. Now I got nothin.'"

He took a step closer and crossed his arms over his chest. "Who's gone?"

"Cecelia. She left. She's gone. My fancy tutor." I hadn't told him about her leaving. Couldn't talk about it. Didn't really accept it was true until today and I saw her get on a plane.

"Where'd she go?"

I looked up at him. "I don't fucking know."

"Why the fuck not?"

"Cuz I'm an idiot. Idgit! Idgit!" I smacked my palm to my forehead. "Can't even write a fucking letter to resign. I *K-W-I-T*. Is that how you spell it? I'm sorry. You trusted me and I failed you."

"Shut the fuck up."

"Like I fail everyone. You can beat my ass. Burn loser into my back. You bring a branding iron?"

"Fucking shit." He pulled out his phone. "Blythe, bad news. Another fire. Province Bluffs. Get insurance rolling and pull Locke off Terrace Heights. Have him send a demo crew first. Then carpenters, roofers, electricians and a finishing crew. Give him three weeks." A short pause. "Thank you." He ended the call and turned his eyes back to me. "You ever had a fire on a jobsite before?"

Three weeks? This Locke person had a huge, multi-talented crew and could rebuild this place in three weeks?

"You ever had a fire on a jobsite?" he repeated.

"Yes. A barn I built burned down. Tessa and I risked our lives to get the horses out. A man died in that fire."

"And did you quit? Which is spelled *Q-U-I-T* by the way."

"Told ya I can't spell for shit."

"Did you quit when your barn burned?"

"No, sir. Rebuilt it in two week's time."

"Right. So you cleared the debris and started over?"

"Yes."

"Makes no difference if your heart is broken or not, you strap on your boots and get to work."

"Yes, but..."

"Listen. I ain't happy my house burned down. You did a great fucking job. It was a beautiful house. But this is not your fault."

"You don't know that."

"I do. This was most likely arson. It's all on me not you. There's a lot of people who don't wanna see me succeed. They burn down my builds all the time." He offered me a hand up.

"You coulda warned me." I took his hand and stood up.

"I gave you the gun."

"You forgot to mention the arsonists!" I brushed the soot from my pants.

"It's only the back half."

"Took me nine months to build this place. You got big crews and let me stand out here all winter working with just four men?"

"You said you wanted to prove yourself on your own merit. You've done that."

"Good. Now what?"

"We rebuild this one. It becomes the model. We build four more on adjacent lots."

"You serious?" He had this planned all along?

"Economy of scale, my friend."

So he was teaching me a lesson? I'd take it. "Alright. I'll be your foreman, you give me as much labor as I want."

"Of course."

"What's your timeline?"

"Three months per house. One year and we're done."

"I'll build you four houses in twelve months. You pay me a million per house. Four million one year from today."

"We can do that."

"And no bringing me into the family. My parole's up in three months, but I'm keeping my nose clean. If there's dirty money building these houses, I don't wanna know about it. We're legit business associates. What you do with your profits is not my concern and vice versa."

"Fair enough."

And with that, I had lost everything and gained so much more all in the blink of twenty-four hours.

Chapter 18

A WEEK AFTER THE FIRE, I set the framed picture of Cecelia and me back on the mantel above the fireplace. The crews had finished clearing the debris and the rebuild progressed fast.

My fingers traced her stunning smile in the picture. She was happy. We were in love. And she still left. She closed the doors and shut me out like the prison guards.

Impossible.

If anyone had asked me a month ago if Cecelia would take off and leave me for another man, I would've said impossible. I knew she had secrets, but I never doubted the love between us.

Nothing made sense. How could this Maksim person have so much control over her that she'd give up everything we had? How was he related to her uncle and her studies at Hale?

Whatever it was, she must be terrified. If she was married and afraid to leave, I wanted to know. Whatever trouble she was in, I wanted to help her. Even if she couldn't be mine, she deserved to be free.

I pulled up the internet browser on my phone and tapped the microphone button which had become my best friend. "Search for Cecelia Boujani."

A few pictures of her at Hale showed up. Nothing else.

Gritting my teeth and sucking up my pride, I called Tessa.

"Hi, Zook." She sounded happy to hear from me. I hadn't seen her since the night at the club when her He-man husband knocked my hat off. Cecelia and her had become friends, mostly chatting about me and my studies. "Cecelia said the mansion you're building is almost done and it's spectacular."

I liked that Cecelia had told her about the build. "It was. Till it burned down."

"Oh no."

"It's alright. We're rebuilding. The journal you gave me was in a fire-proof safe. I still have it." When she was seventeen, she wrote a bunch of shit in a journal and gave it to me. She said if I wanted to know what it said, I had to learn to read. I wanted to know, but I wasn't gonna let her teach me.

"Oh, well. Hmm... You saved that?" Her voice wavered and got quiet.

"Yes. Meant a lot to me. Studied those journal entries every night I was in prison, trying to figure out what you were saying about me. Wasn't until CeCe taught me to read, I could fully understand them. You loved me."

"It was a long time ago," she whispered.

I had her on the hot seat. The words a young girl writes to her boyfriend in her journal. Now that young girl is married to another man.

"Kinda pissed you didn't save yourself for me." I was totally messing with her head. Wanted to see if she still had a sense of humor.

She paused and cleared her throat. "What? We didn't promise each other anything. We agreed to find our lives outside the compound. We both needed someone who grew up in normal society." I was gonna respond, but she was all riled up and she kept talking. "Too many of our memories were tainted and convoluted between reality and craziness. We needed someone who grew up outside if we were gonna have any kinda chance at a normal life."

She was getting upset, but it was too much fun to let her off the hook. "Still, you shoulda waited for me."

"Are you out of your mind? Shut up, Zook. You're teasing me and it's not funny."

I laughed. "It's totally funny. You got all defensive."

"I did not!"

I laughed again. She totally did.

"Is that why you called, to tease me about my old journals?"

I took a deep breath and sucked it up. This was for CeCe. "No. I need to ask your husband for help. I'm looking for Cecelia."

She was quiet for a few seconds. "Is she missing?"

"She went back home after graduation. I just don't know where she went."

It sucked talking about this, but if CeCe needed me, I'd swallow my pride and make it happen.

"She left without telling you where she was going?" She sounded as shocked as I felt.

"Yeah. She had issues with her uncle. I have some serious concerns she's gone back to an abusive situation. It's driving me mad. I gotta do whatever I can to get her out of there."

"Did you try to talk her out of going back?"

"I did. She left anyway."

"Oh no. That sounds bad. I'll ask Rogan to get on it ASAP. Send him everything you know."

"I'll pay his fee."

"He'll do this as a favor to me. Do you have any more information?"

"Just that she graduated from Hale. She got on a Turkish Airlines flight to Moscow. She mentioned a man named Maksim who controls her. I'll send you a picture." I picked up the picture again and studied it for any sign of what the hell was going on. "I got it. Her pendant. Her friend Soraya wore the same one. It's in the picture. Show it to Rogan. See if he can trace it back to her."

"That's a longshot, Zook."

"It's all I have."

"Okay, I'll give it all to Rogan and see if he'll take on the project. Even if we find her, how're you gonna convince her to come back? You know how hard it was with the women from the compound."

"Leave that to me. I know her better than anybody. I'll convince her."

"I hope you find her. I'll do all I can on my end."

"Appreciate it. Uh, can I ask one more thing."

"Hmm?"

"Where's Orion?" My old Appaloosa from the compound. I'd been afraid to ask Tessa before, knowing the odds of her being alive were slim.

"I've been waiting for you to ask me that."

"Why?"

"She's here. In my stable. With Traveler."

"She is?"

"Yes, I've had her since the trial."

"How's she doin'?"

"She's happy. Aged. She hardly leaves the pasture anymore. Stays in the barn all winter. Still stubborn and ornery, like you."

"When I get a place, I want her in my stable."

"She's bonded with Traveler, Zook. You can't separate them."

"Shit. Well, then. I'm glad she has you and Traveler."

"And Rogan and our dog. You can visit her anytime."

"I will. Sounds like she's happy."

"She is."

"And you are too?"

"Yes. Blissfully happy."

"I'm glad. Night, Tessa.

"Night, Zook."

"A FIRE RESISTANT INTUMESCENT cloth patch, sold in square meters, to be applied to ceilings and walls using..."

Blah, blah, blah. Blythe reading plans to me grated my last nerve. Nothing like the patience and sexy rasp when CeCe taught me. Blythe's pleasure in asserting her power over me echoed in every syllable.

My phone lit up with a text from Rogan.

Rogan: May have located your girl

Ten days I'd been checking my phone and heard nothing. Finally, some word. And five of the best words I could've expected.

He sent a link. It led to some website with pictures of oil tankers in a harbor.

"Are you listening, Zook? This fire protection has to be spot-on in case we're targeted again." Blythe needed to shut her mouth right now.

"Yeah, yeah. I got an urgent message."

As the page loaded, I walked away from an indignant Blythe.

A modern office building as big as a shopping mall dominated the homepage. Strobe beams crossed above it and disappeared into the night sky. The logo in the upper left corner matched CeCe's pendant. I'd only just started to learn cursive letters, but now I could clearly make out a script *N* and a *B* twisted inside the circle of gold.

I closed myself into the room CeCe and I used as our bedroom and called Rogan. "What's the story?"

"Found the logo on a company in Central Asia. The *N* and *B* are for Naibu Brahm Oil. Click on the leadership page."

Shit. Fuck. Leadership probably started with an *L*, right?

The first image showed a crusty older man with gray hair. He looked about the same height as the man I saw leave Cecelia's apartment, but I couldn't be sure.

"King Ivan Sharshinbaev is president and CEO of NB Oil," Rogan said, taking pity on me and reading me the names. "Oil mogul. Two point six billion net worth."

"Two billion?"

"Yes. Below him." A younger man who resembled Ivan, but with darker hair. "His son. Prince Maksim Sharshinbaev."

Maksim.

Holy shit. We found him.

In a second picture, Maksim stood at a podium in front of a brand-new oil refinery. Brilliant sterling silver pipes in the middle of a deserted grassland. A hundred men wearing suits gathered around him, but all of their shoulders were noticeably placed below him.

"He's a prince?"

"Purely symbolic. Royalty has been defunct there for years, but yes, King Ivan is remotely related to the last reigning king in the country, and Maksim is first in line to the throne. Ivan has two other sons, Pavel and Yegor."

"Is she royalty too?" Could she really be a princess? She hated it when I called her that.

"I don't know what her role is there. I'm not even sure she's there. No sign of her anywhere."

"But the company insignia matches her necklace?"

"Yes."

"What are the chances? King Ivan looks similar to a man I saw leaving her place once. When she and Soraya left for the airport, they were escorted by two men."

"Those are all good signs. But I'm not sure. Maksim's a fairly common name in that region. There may be a thousand Maksims working for NB Oil. Seems odd for a women to wear jewelry with oil company logos as a fashion statement. It's possible they had her wear that necklace while she was in the States as a way to claim ownership of her."

"Yes. That's what I'm thinking since her roommate wore the same one."

"I wouldn't be surprised. Did she have any tattoos?"

"No."

"I'm gonna ask you something personal, man. But all information is helpful here."

"Shoot." I'd tell him anything if it would help.

"She have any genital mutilation?"

Oh thank God, no. "No."

"Mmm. She could be royalty. Subject to whatever rules they have for their women. Or she could be being forced into some kind of servitude, working for NB Oil."

"Like slave labor?"

He grunted. "Did some research for you. Veranistaad is a tiny country in no-man's land between Russia and Saudi. It's a former Soviet republic. If she's royalty, she's not in the limelight. No pictures of her at social events. But it's not uncommon in that region for women to be bought and sold as property. Forced to work in the sex industry or labor camps."

"If she were a slave, why would her uncle send her to the States for an education?"

"That's why I'm leaning more toward royalty. Sending wealthy children to exclusive private schools would be something they would do."

"Okay so if she is royalty, or being forced into slave labor, could I go there, get her, and bring her back?"

"If you were able to make contact, which would be challenging, I doubt she'd be allowed to leave, especially with an American stranger."

"Yes. This is all making sense now. Shit. How do we reach her?"

He cleared his throat. "I have to step out here. I can't probe into foreign affairs. I walk a thin line with the US government. I keep a low profile, and they leave me to my business."

What? He was backing out on me? How the hell would I get her out of there? "So that's it? You can't help me?"

"No. But you have two other options."

"Okay."

"You can hire Dallas Monroe." Dallas Monroe? Why did that name sound familiar? Was he the big guy who pulled the gun on me the night Rogan hauled me out into the alley? Yes. He said he owned Siege.

Rogan continued. "He runs a private military contractor operation. He could send a team over to find her. It would be expensive, and they may not be able to penetrate their security."

Wow. Dallas was a busy man running a nightclub and a military contractor business. I'd pay his fee though, whatever it took to get her back. "What's the second option?"

"NB Oil has an active request for construction proposal posted on their website."

"A request for bids?"

"Yes. Click on current projects. There's a job for American contractors only."

"Hold on a second." Took me a while, but I found a page called *current projects*. "I see it. Holy shit. Eight million for a palace on a hillside?"

"Yeah. I hear you're working with Torrez Lavonte."

"Yes. You know him?"

"He's an associate of Dallas. Word is Torrez Lavonte could pull off a job of that size and might even be welcomed there by the Sharshinbaev Clan."

Why would the Russians welcome Torrez, the Brazilian from Boston? "Really. Why's that?"

"I can't tell you Lavonte's business. You gotta talk to him. He can advise you whether it would be better to hire him or to go in yourself. My gut's telling me infiltrating as a contractor is your best bet. Dallas and Lavonte might confirm that if you give them all this intel."

So Torrez knew Rogan and Dallas. And I met Torrez right after I showed up at Siege. And Tessa worked at Siege, so she must know Dallas. Rogan wouldn't have sent Torrez to help me, but Dallas might have done it if Tessa asked him. Tessa would absolutely do something like that for me too. So maybe me meeting Torrez wasn't such a coincidence after all.

"I'll do that. Thank you. How much do I owe you?"

"I did this free of charge. My woman asked me to do it and so I did. But I draw the line at crossing borders."

"Appreciate the favor."

I disconnected and called Torrez.

"Zook. Wassup?"

"Rogan tells me you know a man named Dallas Monroe at Siege." I wasn't gonna mess around. I got straight to the point.

The construction sounds in the background became muted like he'd gone inside a room and closed the door. "I know him. Why?" he answered cautiously.

"By any chance did Dallas ask you to hunt down a sorry lookin' schmuck wearing a cowboy hat at a pub in Boston and offer him a job?"

He laughed. "You figured that out, did you?

"I'm thinking Tessa asked Dallas, Dallas asked you, and you needed a foreman anyway, or maybe you owed Dallas something, and you came down to the pub and shot the shit with me for an hour then offered me a job." Jesus, how could I not have seen it before? I was a total charity case. Tessa sent Cecelia to tutor me and Torrez to give me a chance. Well shit.

"It might've happened that way. I'll never admit. But it doesn't matter. I'm happy to have you on the team. You're reliable, smart, and you do good work fast."

This was true. And I liked the compliment.

"You've become a friend too, Zook," he added in a softer voice.

A gust of air zoomed through my throat and I couldn't breathe for a second. I guess I had made a friend in Torrez. "You've become a good friend too, Torrez. At a time when I had none. Appreciate it." I took in a deep breath of air.

"Welcome."

Okay. Now that I got him warmed up. "As a friend, I need a favor."

"What's that?" He sounded distracted and the background noise returned.

"Have you done international work?"

"Some," Torrez answered.

"Ever been to Central Asia?"

"That's a huge region."

"I found a request for proposal in Veranistaad."

"An RFP in Veranistaad? No. I haven't been there." He still sounded indifferent.

"A palace for an oil mogul. Naibu Brahm Oil. You interested?"

"What's the budget?" His voice perked up and the door closed to the noise again. Guess oil was the magic word.

"Looks like about eight million. We get it done Zook style, we could each take home two point five million." I let my excitement show in my voice. It was an amazing project.

"Do we have a chance?" he asked.

"He wants an American contractor," I said. "Don't get more American than a cowboy from Idaho and a retired Navy SEAL." Fluffing his ego a little should open his mind.

"Is there an ulterior motive here?"

"No." I lied.

"Nothing to do with a girl?" He figured me out.

"CeCe is from Veranistaad. Or she may be."

"And you think you'll find her through this job?"

"Her pendant matches the company logo."

"That's all you got?"

"Yeah."

He huffed out a disbelieving laugh. "We're flying across the world to bid on a project because the girl who dumped you might know this guy? And then? We build him a palace, she decides she made a huge mistake and comes running back to you?"

"That's the plan."

He sighed. "So, we're putting our current projects on hold and flying to butt-fuck Egypt for some pussy that may reject you on sight?"

"Yes."

He was quiet in a way I knew he was counting to ten to calm himself. "I'll have Blythe start a proposal package."

"Thank you."

Chapter 19

TORREZ AND I GATHERED our bags as the plane touched down in Portul, the capital city of Veranistaad. After a full-day on airplanes when I'd never flown in one before, I was anxious to get out of my seat.

My first breath of Veranistaad air clogged my throat with super-heated air and a fine layer of burnt sand. The middle of July was the worst time to travel to this region and the air here tasted like poison.

With that breath, I knew one thing; I would not leave this country without CeCe by my side. I could never leave her behind in this desolate place while I flew to freedom and fresh air in America.

A taxi cab shaped like a shoebox took us to the NB headquarters outside Portul. A small man wearing sandals and a white headpiece escorted us into a conference room. "You may leave your hat here."

"Nah, thanks. I'm good." I wasn't taking off my hat for no one.

Torrez smacked my bicep. "Take off your damn hat." He spoke under his breath so only I could hear.

He was right. Anything for her. I set my hat on a small table near the door.

"Prince Maksim will be with you shortly. It is customary to bow to him as he enters the room. You will refer to him as Your Highness."

Memories of bowing to Jeb and calling him Father flashed through my mind. I bow to no one. I honor no self-proclaimed titles. But this was for Cecelia's freedom, so I would grit my teeth and bow to the man.

My eyes scanned the room for any sign of her. White marble covered the floors and purple velvet curtains hung from the windows. Giant swords were crossed in an *X* over the mantel. No women. None.

This was futile. How could taking off my hat and bowing to a prince lead me to her? Impossible.

But if she were here—and she needed me—it would all be worth it.

"No jokes today, Guthrie. The sense of humor is very different here." Torrez had warned me of this many times.

"Got it."

The man I assumed to be Prince Maksim Sharshinbaev walked in and stopped before us. He wore a black suit with a white button-down shirt. Slicked-back dark hair, brown eyes. He looked a little older than in his pictures, but I knew from my research he was twenty-eight. He didn't seem like a bad guy. In fact, he appeared to be pleasant and personable. But looks could be deceiving.

He looked at us expectantly. Torrez and I bowed.

We straightened and he held out his hand to Torrez. "Torrez Lavonte?" Torrez stepped forward and shook his hand. "Pleasure to meet you, Your Highness."

He nodded. "Is this your foreman?"

"Yes. Zook Guthrie. Most skilled contractor you'll ever find." He held out his hand to me. I stepped toward him. I knew assholes like him. A power trip to get me to take the step. Fine. I did it and shook his hand. Soft skin. Weak. The man never worked in the sun a day in his life.

"We have made arrangements for you to stay in a guest apartment at one of our palaces near the site. Electricity has been turned on, and you'll need to drill for water until you connect with the main in the major street." He spoke crisp English with a thick Russian accent.

"Not a problem," I answered. I'd drilled a well for water before. No idea how deep we'd have to go here, but I could handle it.

"You must finish the project in four months. We have a three-day wedding celebration planned there on opening day. You are welcome to stay and attend. It will be a glorious evening."

Four months. I had four months to build this palace and find her. Hopefully it would be before the four months passed because now that I was here, I wanted to see her right away.

But what if the four months passed and I never found her? This whole trip would be such a failure.

Or what if at the end of all this, I found out CeCe was going to be his bride? And I had built the palace he would marry her in and live the rest of his life with her? The odds of it being her were slim. If Ivan Sharshinbaev was her uncle, wouldn't his son, Maksim, be her cousin?

"Fasul Dareem will be your interpreter." Maksim tilted his head toward the man who had escorted us in. The man bowed again. "He can get you any materials you need and relay any questions to me or my father."

Right. So. First order of business, befriend Fasul Dareem and find out who is getting married in four months. Second order, pray like hell it's not Cecelia.

"Come, let us share a drink to seal the deal." He motioned for us to follow him into a room set with platters of ripe fruit, cheese, stews, meats and sweets. He poured us each a shot glass of vodka.

Yes, let's toast, my friend. I keep my enemies close. Tell me all about your little oil company and wedding celebration.

Torrez patted my back with enough pressure to signal I needed to get it under control. I forced my shoulders down and loosened my stance as the clear liquid burned my throat.

Let the games begin.

Chapter 20

FOUR MONTHS LATER

The night of the wedding, the pinned colt inside me was bucking so hard he dented the rails. Four months—no sign of Cecelia. No sign of any women at all associated with the Sharshinbaevs apart from a few servants who cleaned the palace and prepared the interior for tonight.

Fasul confided in me when I asked; the couple getting married was Pavel, Maksim's youngest brother, and a woman named Nariam. I didn't know what name Cecelia went by here, and I couldn't ask Fasul too many questions without drawing attention, but the fact that her name wasn't Cecelia gave me the shred of hope I needed to get through tonight without busting up the walls.

Torrez and I strode through the pristine grand foyer of the palace—the palace built for Maksim by our hands. And holy shit, they'd transformed the thing into a flower garden. Big purple and white puffs covered the walls, the ceiling, and all the surfaces. We walked past a giant white cake as big as my prison cell.

"Take off your hat, Zook." Torrez nudged my arm, still trying to impress Maksim. No way. I'm done with that shit. Maksim wanted American craftsmanship? Well, this American cowboy wears his hat indoors. Deal with it.

Torrez and I wore tailored tuxedos Maksim had arranged for us. My first time in a tuxedo and I was carrying a loaded Sig Sauer nine millimeter in my jacket pocket. One good thing that came out of this trip was the shooting lessons Torrez took me out on every Sunday. I could shoot Maksim from fifty yards if I had to. Hopefully, it wouldn't come to that. But just in case, Torrez made sure to prepare me.

My fists tightened into rocks as we entered the great hall. Mostly men in tuxedos, some wearing a folded white cloth secured with a black rope around their foreheads. Four men sat in a long row of ornate gilded thrones on the stage we had constructed at the front of the room. Ivan presided at the head, looking over the festivities. Maksim, next to him, held a smug grin on his face as he sat next to an empty chair. His brothers, Yegor and Pavel, also had empty chairs next to them. Feminine purple sashes with golden tassels draped under the lapels of their jackets and crossed their bellies. You'd never see me wearing lame shit like that, royalty or not.

But I wasn't here to look at the men. Women topped my priority list tonight. One woman in particular. If Cecelia wasn't here, Torrez and I would be on a plane tomorrow without her. It would cut me to the bone to have made all this effort and go home alone, but if she didn't show up, I had no other leads. Do or die time.

As I scanned the room casually, my hopes plummeted. She didn't fit in with this scene at all. The few women among the crowd wore tacky beaded evening gowns in bright colors. They had fake curls shaped into beehives attached to their heads. Diamonds hung from their wrinkled necks and dipped into their vulgar cleavage. Just goes to show all the money in the world couldn't buy beauty.

She wasn't here. I didn't sense her. My skin didn't come alive like it did when she was near.

"Valued guests!" The murmuring of the crowd quieted and everyone turned their eyes to Fasul holding a microphone and standing at the corner of the stage near King Ivan. "Welcome to the evening all of Veranistaad has been waiting for. Let the celebration commence with the presentation of the bride to the groom!" He spoke in English first, then Russian, then some language I'd heard a few of the staff speaking but didn't catch more info on, but I assumed it was Veranistaadian.

Here we go.

God, if Maksim was marrying Cecelia, Torrez would have to hold me down.

But Maksim didn't stand up. His brother did. Pavel walked to the center of the stage.

"Princess Nariam Ranakova is presented to the His Royal Highness Pavel Sharshinbaev!"

The string quartet in the corner played a grand entrance song, and the crowd clapped and cheered as a girl walked out.

Thank all the fucking stars in heaven. Not her. Much shorter than CeCe and a fairer complexion. Her fluffy white dress looked like it weighed a ton. Her blonde hair stuck up in a shiny ball out of her crown. Heavy makeup concealed the real girl behind all that crap, but she wasn't mine. I was sure of it.

As the wedding couple took their seats, the next brother stood and walked to the front of the stage. "Next please welcome the wife of Prince Yegor Sharshinbaev, back from a long stay in America to finish her master's degree from Hale, Princess Soramina."

Princess Soramina? Soraya? Yes, that was CeCe's friend and her old roommate. I held my breath and the caged colt inside me went ballistic. Torrez shot me a look to remind me of the strategy he planned during our shooting lessons. *Be patient. Wait for the right moment to act. Strike when least expected. At the party, security will be high. We find her and return for her when he's not prepared.*

Soraya's sparkly scarlet dress hugged her figure, a long silver sash hanging from her shoulder. Her lips, painted a bright red, did not smile. She took Yegor's arm, and he guided them to their seats.

Maksim stood and walked to the center of the stage. After a pregnant silence, a collective gasp filled the room as the most captivating creature you've ever seen took the stage. My heart stopped at the first sight of her in six months.

Gorgeous. Cecelia.

My CeCe. I'd found her.

She walked up behind Maksim. I knew what was coming next.

"Also back from the States after earning her master's degree, please welcome the wife of Prince Maksim Sharshinbaev, Princess Celiana."

An avalanche of wet sand slammed down on my head, cutting off air and blinding me.

She's married to him. She's a fucking princess, and she's married to Maksim.

Fucking hell. The worst-case scenario was unfolding before my eyes.

How long had she been...

Was she married when she was with me?

Of course she was.

Married. Celiana Sharshinbaev. Cecelia Boujani.

I haven't slept with him in six years.

She may have been married to him, but she didn't have sex with him, and she didn't love him.

The din of the crowd broke through the mountain of sand encasing me. They smiled and clapped excitedly.

The men's faces changed to envy, greed, lust. The most disgusting of them all was Maksim and his father. They were so proud of their Cecelia. They owned her. She was their prized possession.

I turned my attention back to her. A brilliant tiara perched on her forehead. Her curves were accented in a beaded aqua-marine gown with long sleeves, just a hint of her cleavage showing.

She held a glossy beauty contestant's smile on her face. Plastic and strained. But her eyes always told the story. Unfocused and lifeless. Dead inside. A Veranistaad princess with a soul tied to a little Napoleon.

We made eye contact.

She stood frozen in place.

Yes, baby. It's me. I'm here.

I nailed her gaze from under my cowboy hat.

Her eyes flared and she took a stuttering step back. Her sculpted brows arched, and her lips twisted. Slowly, awareness and tears filled her eyes. Black triangles formed above her cheeks and smeared to her lips like a morose clown. She held her ramrod strict posture but her face gave everything away.

Maksim looked at her for the first time since she'd taken the stage. He squinted and stared at her. He was oblivious to her until she was about to fall apart.

He grasped her bicep and spun her around. No one else could see, but his fingers pinched her hard as he whispered into her ear. She winced and the stiff frame she'd so bravely held up finally broke. Her shoulders collapsed and her hands flew to her face as her body convulsed.

He yanked CeCe off the stage.

She'd ruined his big moment.

He didn't care why she was crying.

And I knew then.

He planned to hurt her.

She'd be punished for this.

His caged bird sang too loudly tonight.

And she'd pay for it.

I had to get to her before he did, but I couldn't run in the crowd or draw attention to her, so I made my way over to the place I saw her leave.

Torrez grabbed my arm. He gave me some *take it easy* crap but I couldn't process his words. She needed me. Nothing else mattered.

Chapter 21

CECELIA

"Celiana, gather yourself."

Maksim's disapproving voice poked my consciousness, but I didn't hear.

Zook?

Surely my imagination had gone rogue.

Zook could not be standing at the edge of the crowd.

His pretty blue eyes couldn't be staring at me from under his Stetson.

After months of not sleeping, constant crying, and dreaming of him, I'd lost my sanity. I couldn't separate reality from fantasy.

With each blink, I expected the mirage to turn to vapor. His stunning face would be replaced with a mean oil crony of Maksim's. I squinted through the haze.

Yes.

It was him.

Zook in all his glory was here. His eyes were on me. Angry and confused, but nevertheless passionately looking at me. He stood in the room with the authority only he could carry. Only Zook would wear a tuxedo and cowboy hat. He'd insist on it.

Zook had found me. He was here for me. To offer a last-minute lifeline in the void of loneliness.

The blood in my veins calcified. Moving became impossible. Every cell in my body ached to run to him, jump in his arms, and kiss every inch of his face. But like always, the concrete block of fear around my feet held me down.

My body was petrified like a tree in an old wood forest. Tears gushed from my eyes like rain, full of regret and longing for the only man I've ever loved.

Maksim's hand pinched my arm and broke through the final bit of self-control I'd managed. I turned my back to the crowd, bent over, and cried into my hands.

Zook had come to save me, and I couldn't go to him. Maksim would kill him. He'd kill me. We couldn't do this.

The pain in my arm became scorching. Maksim's anger leeched off him like fire. "Get off this stage right now, you idiot!" He tugged me and I stumbled. He pulled me off the stage to a small rectangular dressing area behind the curtain. As I straightened, the smack of his palm thumped my cheek. "Gather yourself!"

I rubbed my face and breathed through the shocked numbness as the burn spread out. He hit me? Here?

Maksim never hit me in public. He'd struck my friend Kurt from boarding school in public when I snuck out to meet him in Portul. But my beatings were always behind closed doors.

Tonight, if I didn't stop crying, he'd strike me again. I needed to stop crying, but I just couldn't. Zook came all this way. For me. He saw me with Maksim. Zook had seen me shamed and presented like property. He knew my secret. I'd hurt him and lost him forever.

One, two, three.

Three deep breaths.

Put on a show.

Keep appearances.

Fall apart later.

I straightened my spine and faced Maksim through my tears. "I- I'm so sorry. The emotion of the wedding got the best of me. It's such a glorious day." I wiped my face and sniffed back the tears. And I was honestly sorry. Not that I'd humiliated Maksim and the royal family, but I'd drawn so much attention. My tears made Zook a target.

"It's far too late for apologies. Do you know how much money is on the line here? Investors must see me and my clan as indestructible. You represent the ideal they aspire to be. And they will give me money to try to get there. Yet you weep like a fool in front of them!"

I stared at the floor and dropped my shoulders. I hated him, yet some sick part of me still wanted his approval. What a complete and utter waste of a person I'd become. I never should've dragged Zook into this.

"Are you not happy here? I do not beat you. You are not raped."

He'd warped the truth so much he believed it himself. But the truth was before I left for Hale, he beat me and forced sex on me each time I came home for boarding school on breaks. The intercourse stopped and the beatings became less frequent when I went away to Hale and he trusted me to obey, but that didn't take away the fact it happened.

He pointed his ugly finger at my nose. "You have a world-class education."

That I will never use.

"I gave you a shopping allowance so you could have your couture clothes."

He'd only done that the last two years, probably to appease me because he sensed my independence growing.

"And still you stand before me ungrateful. I saved you from a family who didn't want you. Now you are a princess. I can return you to the streets at my whim."

He used that one all the time because he knew it struck my deepest insecurity. My family had abandoned me. "I am grateful, Maksim. This is my family. I don't wish to leave." It wasn't true, but I knew what I needed to say to mollify him.

"You were always such a good girl. Since you've returned, you've been disobedient."

Since I'd been back, I'd hidden in my room claiming I was ill. I didn't do any work. I ate my meals in my room.

He gripped my arm and squeezed. "You remember how we treat disobedience?"

How could I forget? The image of him and Yegor raping a killing a young girl burned constantly in my brain. It guided all my actions and my choices since I'd witnessed it at age fifteen. Soraya and I were tied to chairs and forced to watch as Maksim and his brothers gang-raped and killed her. She was meant to be Pavel's, but she fought too hard. Even after they raped her, she wouldn't submit. So they beat her to death. I watched her die. Maksim told us it would be us and anyone we got too close to.

"Clean your face and return to the celebration." His eyes scanned me up and down with disdain. "If you can't do that, I don't need you anymore. We'll dispose of you the same way."

I believed him. I believed he'd rape and kill me, and if he knew about Zook, he'd make Zook watch. "Yes, Maksim. Thank you." *Yes* is the only thing he wanted to hear from me.

"You will spend tonight in isolation to ponder what it's like to be alone."

I expected that. I hated and loved isolation. The room had no windows. No one brought me food. It was dark except for a dim bathroom bulb. But Maksim rarely came to visit me when I was in there. So I was safe for a short time.

"Never do this again." He stormed through the curtain to return to the wedding.

"Yes, Maksim." How many times had I said that in my life?

Yes, Maksim.

My mangled reflection in a metal beam holding up the stage startled me.

I'd become a crying, begging hollow of a woman. Where was the woman I was with Zook?

"Psst."

I gasped and turned to the sound of the noise.

Zook held the curtain open and shushed me with his finger. My heart jumped out of my chest. We were so close. The heat of his energy hit me like a force field.

His hand reached for me, cupping the cheek Maksim struck. "Did he hurt you?" he whispered, his eyes glowing a livid dark blue.

My head tilted into his palm.

I placed my hand on his face and caressed the stubble on his chin.

It was the closest to a hug I could risk. And it felt so good. To touch his warm skin. To look into his fierce face and take in his beautiful features one more time. One last time.

"You shouldn't be here." I dropped my hand.

"Yes, I should. I'm here for you."

I knew it. He came all this way for me.

"How did you find me? How did you get into the party?"

"Rogan found you. I built this place."

Oh my god. "You built the new palace?"

"I did. Was looking for you the whole time."

He built this palace to look for me? "No, Zook. Don't do this. Please, don't put yourself at risk for me."

"We are doing this. You don't belong here. You're leaving with me." His hand curled behind my neck and tugged me closer.

Memories of Zook and my love for him pulled me closer. Then the threats ambushed my brain. The gruesome image of the lifeless girl's bloody body on the floor. No. With all my might, I pulled away. "Go. This is so dangerous."

The disappointment in his eyes charred my soul. He expected me to say yes. I wanted to say yes.

"I'm not afraid." He spoke with such confidence. But I knew from a life-time of dealing with Maksim, we couldn't win this one. Not alive.

"Leave now. Don't talk to me again." I hated to say it to him, but nothing had changed. I had to protect him.

I turned and ran from him—the man I love. I ran the other way to save him.

Chapter 22

IN THE SHOWER OF THE isolation room, as I washed the makeup from my face and the spray from my hair, my mind raced through the events of the evening. Zook totally shocked me by being present at the wedding celebration. He just appeared like the magician from our date had teleported him here. At the sight of him, my vacant heart began to beat again. He looked so incredible and confident in a tuxedo. And his signature cowboy hat made me want to smile despite all the chaos around me. I couldn't believe it. Zook came all this way to save me. He worked, building this palace for months, hoping to find me. And what did I do? I ran away.

The moment I left him and returned to the celebration, the change began. I hated the woman I saw reflected in the metal beams of the stage. The woman who was so cruel, she'd hurt the man she loved. The last straw was when Maksim introduced me to Zook, and I had to pretend I didn't know him. Maksim praised my pedigree like I was cattle for sale, and Zook vibrated with barely controlled fury. Zook stalked away, and I knew then.

He'd given up.

I'd lost him forever.

The pain of that knowledge caused my conviction to shift. Like someone had cast a spell on me, suddenly, the reasons I'd pushed him away didn't seem insurmountable anymore.

At that moment, I made the decision; I would never cause Zook pain like that again. Maksim's threats would no longer work on me. Let him beat me. If he tried to kill Zook, I'd kill him first. Anything was better than the abyss in my soul caused by denying Zook's love.

A dark form entered the bathroom, shaking me from my thoughts. I slammed myself into the corner of the shower and ducked down, but there was nowhere to hide. If Maksim was here to punish me further, I had no way to defend myself. But I'd vowed to start fighting back, so I had to think of something. I could scream, but no one would come help. The shadow moved closer to the opaque glass of the shower door. I grabbed my razor and tucked it into my palm. I'd wait until he was vulnerable and slice it over his balls.

The door slid open. My heart thumped against my ribcage as the water fell in my eyes. I covered my breasts with my hands and turned my head down. When he touched my shoulder, I flinched. "Don't touch me."

"Look at me."

Zook's voice? Had he found me again? He hadn't given up? No, of course he hadn't. Zook would never give up on me no matter how badly I treated him.

I looked up at Zook standing naked in front of me. My eyes traced from his toes, up the hair of his strong muscular legs, his cock, not hard but growing thicker. The sculpted muscles of his abdomen leading to his broad chest and manly spattering of hair there. Everything tight, bulging, and intense.

When I got to his face, I saw his brow drawn through the drops of water that fell from his hair, his gaze steady on me.

He offered me a hand. A lifeline. I took it. I finally took it and it felt right. Zook filled the holes in my heart and I took his hand.

"Stand up, darlin'." His voice felt like a warm raincoat, reaching me through the middle of a storm.

I dropped the razor, and he helped me stand up. His arms wrapped behind my back, smashing my front up against his in a wet smack. He gazed at me for a moment before his lips crashed onto mine. Our mouths opened, his tongue dug in and god, god, it was divine. My fingers slid over his slick chest, clawing at his massive shoulders, trying to pull him so close, he'd never leave.

He ended the kiss and peered down at me. "You're married to him?" A muscle ticked in his jaw, and his hands were rough on my hips.

"Yes." I looked to the side, unable to handle the power of his gaze.

"You don't love him," he said, rather than asked as he tipped my head up to look at him again.

"No. I don't love him. Never did." He needed to know. I didn't love Maksim. Please, believe me.

He nodded like he expected me to say that. "Why are you married to him?"

Oh boy. Time to come clean. God, this was humiliating to admit. I'd never told anyone before. Not even Soraya. But Zook had earned my trust, and I owed him this. I took a deep breath and closed my eyes as I spoke. "Ivan purchased me for him. To play the role of his wife." There. Now he knew the truth.

My eyes opened in time to watch his head snap back and his eyes flare an even more brilliant blue. He shook the water from his head and growled. "He purchased you?"

"For Maksim. Ivan forced me to marry him when I turned fifteen." I pushed the hair back from my face and tried to focus on him through the pending tears, the noise of the shower, and the loud thumping of my heart. What if Zook rejected me? What if Maksim was right? No one else would want me.

"Does he force you to sleep with him?" His voice broke.

"No. Not anymore. Not for many years. It's all fake. To impress his oil friends."

He kissed down my neck and back up to my lips. "God, you're so beautiful. Damn, I love you. I would never force you to do anything you didn't want."

My tears mixed with the water. "I know. I know. You don't need to say it."

"You don't want to stay with him." Again, he stated rather than asked because he knew me.

"No. God. No. I don't. I hate him."

"And you still love me." His deep words rumbled from the back of his throat.

I nodded and clutched his shoulders. I loved him more than life itself. I wanted to be with him. I'd give anything to be with him. I need to say it. He needed to hear it. "I love you. I've always loved you. I never stopped. I'm so sorry I hurt you. I hurt us. I was scared. Trying to protect you from all this."

"I know." He pressed his lips to my ear and tightened his arms around me. "We both made mistakes. I never should've let you leave."

"There were guards at my apartment after graduation. I had no choice."

"It was all fucked up. We're together now. Will you fight for us? Don't let fear stop you. Because we can win. I promise you. Say it. Say you'll fight for us."

The warm water collected in the places we were pressed hard together.

I looked up at him and hoped he saw the honesty in my eyes. "I will."

"You will?" It hurt that he was surprised by my answer, but I guess I deserved that after saying no for so long.

I nodded quickly. "I'll fight for you. I'll fight for us." It felt good to finally say the words that would empower me.

"You won't be afraid?"

Yes, time to be brave. No more crying and hiding. "I will. I love you. I want to be with you. I'm sorry I waited so long. I need you. I want you. I'm ready."

"God yes, CeCe. Yes. Finally. Trust me. I'll get you out of here." Triumph, hope, and relief filled his words and his eyes.

"He's dangerous. He'll kill you without blinking. I've seen him murder a girl with his bare hands. He gets away with it too. No one holds him accountable for anything."

"I can defend myself. But promise me, if I tell you to run, you'll run. If I need to shoot Maksim, you let me."

"I promise. Just be careful."

"I will. We'll make it through. Together." Our hands roamed all over, touching and re-memorizing every bend and curve.

His hard cock pressed against my belly. I gripped it in my hand, tugging hard.

"God. Fuck." He kissed me deep, our tongues dancing and reaching. My body burned for him. My Zook. I needed him in me now. To reconnect. To feel whole again.

He walked us backward, and my spine hit the wall as he lifted my leg behind the knee, arching it up over his hip. Staring into my eyes, he guided his cock in. We both groaned and grunted as he sank in deeper, too much. It meant too much to me, to him. It meant everything. He kept his fiery gaze on my face, watching as I closed my eyes and let Zook overtake me. He seated himself deep inside me.

"You feel that? You feel me? This is where I belong." His voice was scratchy, his breaths short.

"Yes. Yes." He pumped into me hard and fast. I threw my head back, slamming it against the shower wall. His hand came up and cupped my head, protecting me.

The water coated us and hid us from the outside world. We were wet and alone in our slick bubble of ecstasy.

"God. So good. You drive me fucking insane. You're mine. You come for me. You live for me. No one else." I loved the rawness of his voice. It was primal the way he expressed his need to claim me.

"Yes." I could barely speak through my harsh breaths.

His abdomen smashed my clit relentlessly, and his cock massaged all my sensitive spots, sending tremors through my whole body. My climax welled deep, and my spine tingled. Pleasure surged through me as I spasmed around his dick, welcoming him home. He pressed his mouth to mine, and I gobbled him up as he grunted out his release. It felt like our orgasms went on forever. It was pure bliss connecting with Zook again. The way it should be. The emptiness in my heart disappeared. Only the fullness of Zook remained as we clung to each other.

Chapter 23

ZOOK

Holy shit. That was incredible. Totally worth the trip, the stress, everything was worth the price of making love to Princess Celiana. She sighed and collapsed in my arms. Wrapping her in a towel, I pressed my lips to her forehead and helped her out of the shower stall.

As I dried her face and shoulders, red marks on her arms caught my eye. I lowered the towel to see the rest of her. Damn. Imprints from my hands and fingers covered her ribs, her ass, her neck. "I was rough with you in there. You okay?"

"I'm more than okay. I'm delirious right now." She smiled her blissed-out grin.

Good then. Mine. My mark belonged on her, and I enjoyed seeing it on her skin.

"I like you like this." I ran the towel down to her feet. "No makeup, relaxed, naked." Then up again to her shoulders. Felt so good to have her again and give her that sated smile I loved so much.

She hummed her thank you and rested her hands on my shoulders. "How'd you get in?" She opened her eyes and looked around the bathroom, awareness of what we had done probably creeping in now.

"The rooms on this floor all have a second concealed entrance in the back wall. You can get in through the garage."

"You could've been seen." Yes, panic was setting in.

"No one saw me." Actually, Fasul had seen me sneak in after the party ended. I gave him a pleading nod. Shocked the hell outta me when he turned his back, allowing me to proceed without creating an issue. My plan to befriend him must have worked. "We're safe for now. Brave, remember?"

She nodded and chewed her trembling lip as she gripped her towel.

I dried off and pulled on my briefs. "When's Maksim coming back?"

"I don't know. He's out drinking with Pavel and Yegor. He could come back anytime."

I needed to get her out of here fast. Torrez' plan to wait for the right moment bit the dust when I saw her last night. No sitting around doing surveillance. No leaving her behind at his mercy. The time to strike was now while Maksim and his brothers were out drinking.

"How did you travel to the US? A student visa?"

"No. I have an American passport under the name Cecelia Boujani. I don't know if the passport is real or not, but I travel as an American."

"Where is it?"

"Maksim keeps it in a safe. We can't get to it. Why?"

"We're going back to Boston, and you need it to travel."

Shock and excitement passed through her face. "Really?"

"And the safe isn't a problem. I memorized the lock combinations when I installed them."

"Ooh, clever."

Always made me chuckle when my Ivy League tutor thought I was the clever one. "Pack a bag. Get dressed. We'll get the passport and sneak out the secret corridor."

She frowned as she peered into the bedroom. "This is an isolation chamber. I only have my sleep clothes and slippers. Or my dress and heels from last night?"

Isolation chamber? My fists clenched and twitched, aching to punch the wall. My hatred for Maksim grew stronger with each new bit of info she revealed.

I took a deep breath and focused on right here and now. "Wear your sleep clothes. We'll buy you whatever you need at the airport."

She nodded and raced out of the bathroom to dress.

My phone buzzed in my pocket as I slipped on my tuxedo shirt. Probably Torrez.

Nope. Not Torrez.

A text from Fasul.

Fasul: Maksim has returned to the property.

Shit. When Fasul saw me last night, he must've figured out my plan to rescue her. The text meant she had told him who I was to her and he supported us together.

Me: Distract him for me?

Fasul: I try.

Me: Thank you. You love her too?

Fasul: Yes. Very much. Take care with her.

Of course he loved her. Everyone who met her loved her. I liked that she'd spoken so well of me to him that he would risk his job, and possibly his life, to help her escape.

Okay. Shit. So Maksim was here. I had to get her out unnoticed. My brain struggled to think rationally through all the adrenaline and fear. What if Maksim or the guards caught us? We'd both be dead or stuck here as prisoners. What if I had to shoot Maksim? I'd enjoy it, but I'd be no good to Cecelia from behind bars.

Stop. No fear. If I asked Cecelia to be brave, I needed to do the same. I had an unexpected ally in Fasul. And a Navy SEAL in my back pocket if I needed him. I could do this.

Cecelia returned to the bathroom wearing an off-white linen shirt that hung to her knees, cream-colored pants, and white satin slippers. She'd pulled her wet hair into a shining ponytail. She looked beautiful. Any other time, I'd make a point of letting her know, but not right now.

"Did you tell Fasul about me?"

She blinked then admitted, "Yes. I trust him."

"Good, because Maksim is here and we're making a run for it. Fasul's going to distract him for us."

I checked my gun chamber and held the Sig in my right hand.

She winced at the gun, but then squared her shoulders. "I'm ready."

I kissed her hard on the mouth. She laughed. "What was that for?"

"I'm so impressed with you right now."

Her lips quirked into a smirk. "I'm running away in my pajamas. Be impressed when we make it out safely."

Shoot. Right. "Okay. There are two safes. One in the master bedroom suite, one in the trophy room."

Maksim had built a museum-like hall with display cases for his royal crap, his elephant heads, whatever the hell he wanted to show off. The biggest safe in the palace hid in the wall of that room.

"He collects things," she said.

"Including people?" I asked her.

She grabbed my arm like I was on to something. "Yes."

"The trophy room." We both spoke at the same time.

"Let's go. Stay close behind me."

AS WE RAN THROUGH THE passageway, I gripped my phone in one hand, my gun in the other. Took forever for the call to Torrez to connect.

"What?" Fucker answered right before the call went to voicemail. He wouldn't want to hear the pissed-off message I'd leave if he didn't answer.

"Meet us at the airport. We need to get out of the country right now." My breathing became ragged as we rushed down the dark corridor toward the trophy room.

"The fuck?" I'd never heard Torrez sleepy and confused before. Always the man in control.

"First flight out to anywhere but here."

He grumbled and rustled around. "There a reason you can't stick to the plan?"

"I won't leave her here. I'll tell you more later. Right now I need a car. I'm going to steal one from the garage." I'd never stolen a car before, but hopefully Maksim kept some royal keys in there.

"Shit." More clothes rustling. "And is she ready to run?"

"Yes. She wants to be with me." It felt good to say it to Torrez, knowing it was true. "She's brave."

"Good to hear. Makes all this bullshit worth it." Torrez had sacrificed a lot for this mission. Four months away from his kids. He made several million in profit—as did I—but still, he did this for me as a favor. Torrez was probably the only legit friend I had right now.

"Yep. Can we quit the chattin' like girls, so I can get her the hell out of here?"

"Sure." His voice wavered, and he dragged out the word. "Meet me in the parking garage in fifteen minutes. I'll have a car," he said with more confidence.

He'd have a car? Here? "Alright."

He ended the call before I could ask him how he'd get here so fast from the apartment we'd been staying at.

I pocketed my phone and tugged Cecelia's hand. "We have to hurry."

"What about Soraya?" She planted her feet, and I lost hold of her hand.

Shit. I didn't plan for Soraya. I didn't expect to find Cecelia at all, much less her roommate from Hale. Fasul could only hold Maksim for so long. We couldn't risk a side trip to get Soraya. I turned to face her in the dark passageway. "There's no time. We need to go now." We both sucked in quick breaths, trying to regulate our breathing.

She resisted another tug on her hand. "She's my sister."

"Listen, let's get you to safety first. Then we'll make a plan for Soraya." We'd have to come back for her. Torrez would help me come up with a plan.

"Let's sneak in her room and get her," she whispered in a conspiratorial tone.

Okay, Cecelia was taking this whole being brave idea to extremes. "I love that you wanna fight for her too, but first save yourself. For once, fight for you."

She gave me a reluctant nod, and we continued running through the corridor. The house staff hadn't woken up yet. We exited the corridor and ran down the hall to the trophy room.

I guided her to the wall safe and entered the combination. The door clicked open and she smiled. The safe held rolls of cash in all different currencies. Handguns. And passports. Lots of passports. I found hers and stashed it in my jacket pocket. Bingo.

Male voices reached my ears from the hallway. It sounded like they were arguing in Russian.

"It's Maksim and Fasul," Cecelia whispered.

Shit. Fuck. We were cornered. Okay, maybe Torrez knew what he was talking about with his waiting to strike crap. With nowhere to hide, I pushed her behind me, holding the gun at my back.

Maksim walked in and glared at us. Fasul was on his heels, his hands fussing. Maksim's hair was messed up, his shirt untucked, a shadow of a beard appearing on his normally smooth skin.

"What the hell?" His speech dragged and his eyes moved slowly from her to me. Good. Drunk Maksim would be easier to subvert. "Celiana? Why are you in here with him?"

"I know him. From Hale. He's..."

"I love her and she's leaving with me." I made it clear with my tone he should talk to me and not her.

"You love her? Leaving? With you?" His brows drew together in one long caterpillar. He laughed then barked out a string of Russian directed at Cecelia. I felt her recoil behind me. I didn't need to know what he was saying, I could guess he was spewing the words he used to control her. Damn him for making her feel that way.

Cecelia swallowed loudly before she stepped out from behind me and faced him. She answered him in Russian, using her stern teacher voice.

"Fasul, translate for me." I wanted to hear every word of Cecelia finally standing up to him.

"Maksim asked her if it was true and she declared, yes, she loves you." Fasul grinned and nodded at Cecelia, encouraging her and clearly as proud of her as I was.

Maksim grimaced and spoke more harsh words in Russian, directly to Cecelia again, pissing me off more.

Fasul translated for me. "He says you are a felon."

Cecelia snapped back in English. "I don't care. I love him and I'm leaving with him."

Maksim narrowed his eyes and spoke more softly, again in Russian.

Fasul hesitated.

"Tell me, Fasul," I said.

Cecelia translated. "Maksim said Fasul told him you read like a child."

Oh did he? I spoke directly to Maksim. "Cecelia tells me you have the penis of a child."

Fasul gasped and covered his mouth to hide his amusement. Maksim's jaw set and his eyes flared. It was just a guess, but it looked like I was right.

"She's my property." Finally, Maksim spoke to me in English. His voice became high-pitched as he struggled to control his temper. "I've invested a lot of time and money in her. You can't take her. She belongs to me." His fists shook. Not fun losing, is it, Prince Maksim?

"She's not property. She's a human being and she has a right to be free." My words hung in the air between us. He couldn't deny he'd stolen her freedom.

"She's a whore and a traitor. You shame the whole family if you do this, Celiana. I'll kill you and him." Maksim pressed his lips together and puffed out his chest. "Fasul, call Oleg."

I dropped Cecelia's hand, preparing to reveal my weapon. "No, Fasul. Don't call Oleg."

Fasul didn't move.

"Fasul, call Oleg!" Maksim spit when he talked. Fasul pulled his phone but I could bet he wasn't waking up Oleg. He was on our side. I pulled my gun and aimed it at Maksim. "Go ahead, make a move. I'd love to shoot you right now."

A flash of brown hair brushed in front of me. What the hell? Cecelia screamed and ran forward, raising an old-fashioned dagger above her head. Holy shit. Where the hell did she get that thing? She must've pulled it off the wall.

I ran after her but couldn't stop her. She was already half the distance to Maksim. All I could do was move closer. I got within ten feet and stared in horror as she reached him.

In one swift move, he grabbed her wrists and ripped the dagger from her grip, catching her around the neck and turning her to face me. His eyes darkened, and he held her in a way I could tell he was accustomed to subduing women this way. For the first time, I saw Maksim's true evil side. All his royal composure fled and the controller appeared. He handled many women this way. Bastard.

She struggled and grunted, trying to break his hold. He pulled the dagger up under her neck with one hand, his other braced across her chest. The terror in her eyes burned inside me. He had my girl at his mercy and I couldn't shoot. Damn. Fuck. I couldn't fucking shoot. He knew it. Her body was in front of his and their heads were inches apart.

"Stop," Maksim said to me as I stalked closer. I made it within five feet, my gun still aimed at his head. If she could just break free and get clear I could shoot the asshole and we'd be out of here.

"Let her go, Maksim. It's time. Let her go."

She kept fighting even with the blade at her neck. "Shut up, bitch." He growled and struck her temple with the butt of the dagger. She went limp in his arms. He propped her up in front of him like a shield. With his eyes on me, he raised the dagger and...

God, no!

Plunged it into her stomach.

"No." I jumped and landed on them, pushing her unconscious body out from under his arm.

My gun slipped from my grasp and skid on the tile. Maksim moved to get it but I was quicker. I got hold of it and, with shaking hands, pulled the trigger. The shots echoed loudly through the halls of the palace. I hit Maksim once in the chest. Once in the forehead. He fell to the ground, his eyes wide, his mouth open. His body jolted a few times and I watched his eyes roll up and blood spill from his chest.

I'd never killed a man before, but I was surprisingly calm. Maybe because I'd imagined shooting him just like this with every shot at the driving range. All the practice made the real thing easy. He would never touch her again. Maksim's tyranny ended today at my hands.

"Go!" Fasul pointed down the hallway. "Oleg would hear the gunshot. You must run!"

I scooped up Cecelia's motionless body and nodded at him. "If anyone asks what happened..."

"I will tell them there was an intruder who escaped. I will cover for you. Just go."

"Thank you."

I bolted down the hall to the door to the garage.

Chapter 24

WE BURST THROUGH THE side door and ran between the rows of luxury cars. The main garage door opened and, in the driveway, Torrez hunkered down behind the trunk of the Mercedes we'd rented for the party.

I ran to far side of the car and stopped, trying to catch my breath so I could speak. "She's hurt. He hit her and stabbed her."

He looked us over quickly. "Put her in the back. You drive. I'll help her." Torrez tipped his head to the front of the car. "Keys in the ignition. It's running."

Thank God and all that was holy for Torrez. I positioned Cecelia's limp body in the rear passenger seat, trying to be gentle but also rushing to get the fuck out of here. Her neck twisted at an awkward angle, her face was pale. Blood seeped into her nightshirt at her waist. "Hold on, baby. Don't leave me."

I closed her door and hopped into the driver's seat. "Get in, Torrez."

"One second." He stayed crouched behind the car, his gun still trained on the garage side entrance.

"What are we waiting for?"

The door opened and a big bald dude carrying a gun ran out. Torrez fired one shot and the guard hit the ground. "That. There's only one guard on duty right now, and we just neutralized him." He popped the trunk and grabbed something before he slid into the back seat. We tore down the drive and flew through the front gate of the palace.

"Is she okay?" My voice was wild, my breath ragged and forced. "There's a lot of blood."

"I can see that. How many times was she hit?"

"Once. A knife to her stomach. A blow to her head with the handle of the dagger."

Torrez lifted her shirt and found the spot. "He hit bone. Just tore a lot of skin. I can see her hip bone."

"You can see her bones? Fucker. I killed him, Torrez. I shot him in the chest and the forehead like we practiced."

"Good. If he did this to her, he deserved it. She's unconscious but breathing steady. Pulse slow, but strong. Let me see if I can stop the bleeding." He opened a plastic case he had pulled from the trunk.

"Should I drive to the airport? What do we do?"

He looked out the back window. "Did anyone else see you?"

"No, just Fasul. He helped me. He won't tell anyone."

"Drive toward the airport. We'll stop at a hotel."

I took the road I vaguely remembered leading to the airport. "How is she?"

"She looks okay. Probably a concussion. We need her to wake up."

———————————

WE FOUND A HOTEL BY the airport and brought Cecelia in. I lay her on the bed and Torrez checked her again. Her face had no color, so lifeless, I wanted to scream. He lifted her top and covered her with a towel from the bathroom. The first bandage he'd applied had soaked through with blood. He removed it and worked on applying a new one.

"Why isn't she waking up?"

"I don't know. Give it some time."

"I hate seeing her like this. Fuck." I paced to the window and looked out. "No one followed us."

"Good. So fill me in. What happened?"

"Maksim went out drinking with Yegor and Pavel after the party. I went to her room. She told me everything, and we made a run for it. We ran into Maksim. She charged him with a fucking dagger off the wall. You shoulda seen her, Torrez, she was insane. He used her as a shield so I couldn't shoot him. She kept fighting, and he knocked her out with the handle of the dagger. When he stabbed her, I rushed him, got her away, and shot him. Fasul said he'd cover for me."

"Good job. And what did you find out about him and Cecelia?"

Oh man. "Didn't I tell you over the phone?" I could swear we talked about it.

"No. You said she wanted to be with you and you needed a car. That's all I know."

I ran my hand through my hair. "Sorry, Torrez. We were in a hurry."

"So, tell me now."

I took a deep breath. "Ivan purchased Cecelia as a child and groomed her to be the perfect princess you saw last night."

He froze solid. "The fuck?"

"Ivan bought CeCe and forced her to marry Maksim when she was fifteen. She's American. Her parents sold her to Ivan."

Torrez' mouth dropped open as I spoke. "Soraya."

"Likely the same story. We'll have to ask Cecelia the details when she comes to but..."

"Ivan forced her to marry Yegor." Torrez finished my thought.

"I'd assume so."

He stood and stalked to the window, letting out a series of curse words in English which morphed into Portuguese or maybe Spanish. I couldn't tell. He went on for a long time. I kneeled next to Cecelia and held her hand. Why wasn't she moving at all?

"C'mon, baby. Wake up. We're free. You just need to wake up." I pressed my forehead to her neck. "If God takes you from me now, I won't survive it. Please, baby. I love you so much." I kissed her. Her lips mashed down, soft and fragile like a child's. I kept my mouth there and exhaled as if I could breathe life into her like magic. "C'mon. Come back to me."

Something moved against the back of my head. Either Torrez was getting frisky, or she just touched my hair. I pulled back to see her hand hit the bed again. "That's it. Wake up. It's me. It's Zook. I love you, and I'm here and I need you to open your eyes." I kissed her again and her lips moved, answering mine. "Yes, baby. Good. All the way. Open your eyes."

And she did. Her pretty brown eyes blinked open. My heart started beating, and my lungs sucked in air again. "Yes! Welcome back. We did it. Are you okay?

"I think so."

"You're free."

"Free?"

"He's dead."

"Maksim is dead?"

"I shot him. Twice. He is dead. Never hurt you again."

Her lips quirked up at the corners. "I didn't get to see it."

I laughed. "No, you didn't get to see it. But he's dead. Trust me."

"Mmm."

Torrez returned to the side of the bed and checked her out. "How do you feel? Can you see us okay? Do we look blurry?"

"I see Zook and you perfectly clear. I can't believe you're here, but I see you." Her hand moved to her temple. "Ow."

Placing my hand over hers, I caressed the spot too. "He hit you with the butt of the dagger. It's going to hurt for a while."

She nodded.

"Take these." Torrez handed her some aspirin, and I helped her with a glass of water.

Her eyes looked beyond us and scanned the room. "Where are we?"

"We're in a hotel in Portul near the airport. I'm filling Torrez in on everything that happened with you and Soraya then we need to get going."

"I'm going back for her." Torrez stood up and stared down at Cecelia.

"Now? What's up with you and her?" I asked him.

He turned his steady gaze on me. "When you called me, I was in her room."

"What?" Cecelia and I asked in unison.

"After the wedding celebration, I fucked her."

"You did?" Holy shit. I didn't see any of that happening. I was so focused on Cecelia.

"Yeah. But I didn't know the whole story. I thought, but I wasn't sure. Damn. Why the fuck did I do that?" Torrez pinched the bridge of his nose.

"Do what?" Cecelia asked.

"I said stupid shit to her. Bad shit. Exactly what I shouldn't have said. Thought she set me up. I'm going back to get her. She might not want to leave with me after the load of crap I laid down. Fuck!"

"Let's make sure Cecelia is better and safe here. Then I'll go back with you for Soraya." Torrez helped me get Cecelia back, and now it was my turn to return the favor.

He glanced from me to Cecelia. "No. You both go. Get her home."

I wanted that more than anything, but if he needed me I would stay and help. "You sure?"

"I'm already formulating a plan."

"I'm sure you are."

AN HOUR LATER, CECELIA was recovering quickly, and we caught her up on all that happened while she was out.

"Are you feeling well enough to talk about Soraya? Any info we give to Torrez will help him."

She nodded and spoke softly. "Ivan told her she was adopted, but I don't know if it's true. I saw him hand my parents money for me. They were drug addicts. I was worthless to them. They sold me. Money was more important to them than their own child."

Shit. "God, CeCe. You know that's not true, right?"

She shook her head. "I was old enough to understand what happened. I was ten. They gave their daughter away to strangers and shot the money up their arms."

Torrez stood and walked away. I pulled her closer. "Hey. Don't believe it. What they did says nothing about your worth, okay?"

She closed her eyes, but not sure if she accepted my words. "There was a woman here. Ivan's wife, Nadya. Ivan said she wanted girls. She had three boys, and we were her special girls. The boys were away at boarding school. She taught me Russian and Veranistaadian. It wasn't bad."

Torrez came back, looking slightly more relaxed but still tense. "Where is Nadya now?"

She sighed. "She died. That's when everything changed."

"How'd it change?" My hand rubbed her back, encouraging her to keep going.

She took a deep breath and her voice was small. Damn Maksim for taking her confidence like he did. "Ivan sent us to boarding school in

France. When we came home for the summer, the boys were here too. He said they weren't our brothers. They would be our husbands."

"Shit." Torrez paced away again and came back.

"We were scared. Afraid to fight it. Anytime Soraya resisted, they beat us both, said we were shaming the family. Ivan took all our stuff away and said if we cooperated, we could go back to France. We had more freedom in France at the boarding school. They tracked our phones. Only came for surprise visits."

"So you cooperated?"

"Yes. I was only fifteen when I married him. Soraya was seventeen when she married Yegor. We hated it, but we put up with it so we could keep going to boarding school. He sent us to London for high school. We only had to come home for Christmas and summer breaks. They'd use that time to train us. Maksim started training me when I was sixteen. Ivan instructed him what to say and do to make me submit."

Oh god. "Can you tell us about the training?" My muscles had drawn so tight, the tiniest pressure would cause them to snap, but I held it all in so she could get it out.

She sniffled. She hadn't cried yet, and I was impressed as hell. "Beatings, isolation. I submitted fairly fast. Soraya got the worst of it from Yegor. The scariest part was when they forced us to watch them rape and kill a girl who wouldn't agree to marrying Pavel."

"Goddamn, fuck." Torrez paced and cursed in whatever language again.

"And did you try to escape?" I asked her softly.

She nodded. "Once we went to the police. They recognized us and laughed at us. Ivan has so much influence here, no one would ever accuse him of anything."

"Holy hell." I loosened my arm around her. Didn't want to crush her. "I'm so sorry. If I'd known this, I never would've let you get on that plane."

"There were guards. After the graduation ceremony, I wanted to run to you, but Maksim had guards escort us from our apartment to the air-port. Maybe he knew we would try to escape."

Torrez kept his face stoic as he listened, but his eyes burned with fury.

"In the States, we left once, went to a woman's shelter. We had no mon-ey. Couldn't bring our phones. We used our credit cards to withdraw cash and Maksim had men find us within a day. After that, I decided I wanted to finish my degree, so I could support myself after I escaped. Soraya always wanted to run, but she wouldn't leave without me. That's why I felt so terrible leaving without her this morning."

I'd had enough for now. Torrez had what me needed. "Okay, baby. We'll talk more later. You did a good job telling us what happened."

"Thank you for sharing that with us," Torrez said to Cecelia. "I'll get her out."

"I'm sure you will. This will all work out." Her new strong voice made her so much more attractive than she ever was, and she was a knockout before.

"Yes." I kissed her and rubbed her back.

Torrez looked at his watch and angled his head toward the door. "If you're well enough, we should get you on a plane. We'll stop and get clothes for you both, and I'll drop you off at the airport."

"Thank you, brother." I gave him a hug and a strong arm smack. "Good luck with Soraya."

Chapter 25

THE CAB DRIVER IDLED his taxi in front of the porch of the house in Province Bluffs. He made eye contact with me in the rearview mirror. "Fifty-four seventy-five."

The total reminded me of the cashier the first time we ate at the Hale bistro.

Fifty-four bucks seemed like a lot of money back then.

I edged out from under CeCe's sleeping body and exited the cab. After helping the driver stack our luggage on the drive, I handed him a hundred. "The change is for you."

"Thank you, sir." He pocketed the bill and sat back down in the driver's seat.

I'd never get used to someone calling me sir, but it was happening all the time lately. Must be getting old. Or rich. That's it. Once you're rich, people start calling you sir.

CeCe stirred and her eyes fluttered open as I cradled her in my arms and carried her to the porch. "Are we home?"

We'd been traveling almost a full day. We bought clothes at the airport before the flight and threw our bloody clothes in the airport trash. "Yes. Go back to sleep."

"I want to see it. Put me down."

I set her down and made sure she was stable on her feet. She looked around the grand entrance in awe. "I can't believe it burned down."

"Believe it. On graduation day. That day sucked." Worst day of my life, the day she left me and this house burned down. Best day of my life, apart from getting her back, was the day Torrez sold me the house. I owned it. Mine.

"And you rebuilt it?"

"With the help of a shitload of specialty crews Torrez never told me about."

"And now it's yours?"

"It's ours."

We walked inside and she took a moment to look at the photo of us at the magic show. "You saved it?"

"Yep. Pissed of a few firemen who tried to stop me." I saved her ring too, but we'd get to that later.

"Let's go see the view from the turret." She was already on her way to the stairs. "Is Destry here?"

"No, he's in California working on an album."

I scooped her in my arms and carried her the four flights to the turret. I set her down so she could look out the window. The sun was high and reflected like ice on the surface of the water.

"I remember the first time we came here," she said.

"I remember the first time *you* came here." She blushed. "God, babe. It was a beautiful sight. Your sweet taste on my lips." The first time I had her on my bike. The house was just a frame. I was sleeping on a mattress on the floor. I told her I'd been convicted of rape, and she didn't flinch. The adoration in her eyes never wavered. She listened to my side of the story like I had any right to even tell my side. That first kiss was it for me. "We barely knew each other then, but I knew I wanted you to be mine. Wanted to know the secrets you were keeping."

"Now you know."

"Yes."

"And you still love me?"

"God, yes."

"And you forgive me for leaving you? I did it to protect you."

"I know. I forgive everything. Clean slate. Don't even ask me that. We're here now. Our love is based solely on us. You and me. Nothing could make me stop loving you."

I pressed my front to her back, taking her hand and wrapping her up in my arms. She gazed through the stone arch at the marbled sky in its never-ending dance with the ocean.

"You're free, babe. You flew away," I whispered in her ear. "You never have to go back."

Her shoulders drew forward and her neck went slack. Her breathing stopped and I braced for the tears that always tore me apart. But they didn't come. She turned and her eyes glowed bright as she peered up at me. "If Ivan or Yegor come for me, I'll kill them. I need a gun. And some shooting lessons."

My chuckle rumbled in my throat. "I will protect you, but if you'd like, you can take some training and carry a weapon. If you're well enough, we should travel for a few weeks while I get the security boosted on this place."

"I'm fine, but more travel? We just got here?"

"We need some time for the dust to settle. Won't take any chances with you, and I want you to feel safe here."

"What about Soraya?"

"Torrez seemed to have that under control."

She clapped her hands. "I'm so excited for her. Okay. What do we do now?"

I actually hadn't thought of what we'd do first. "We could unpack..."

"Let's go to bed." She smiled and pressed her body up to mine.

"You're injured. We should..." She tugged at the collar of the button-down shirt we'd bought for me at the airport in Portul, growling when the buttons wouldn't cooperate. "Wait."

"Not waiting. I'm fine." She worked the shirt over my shoulders and licked my chest. "Mmm." She purred like a kitten and bit my nipple. I laughed and my dick filled, ready for action. Oh yeah, loved the new Cecelia.

"You wanna ride me, we're gonna need a bed."

After a quick glance at the slate tile on the floor of the turret, she grabbed my hand, and yanked me down the stairs behind her. With the shirt hanging from my shoulders, we scaled the steps. As soon as we cleared the door to the master bedroom, she kissed me again. "Missed you. So much."

I pulled my arms through the sleeves and yanked them inside out. Shaking my hands did shit to get them off. "I'm stuck in this thing."

She grumbled and burrowed under the shirt to dig into the sleeve from the other side. Her fingers worked the cuffs, and I pulled my arm free. She scurried over to the other side to work the other button. I chuckled because she was so eager to ride me, I was standing there with a huge hard-on, and we couldn't even get our clothes off.

"Don't laugh," she said from under my shirt as her fingers worked on the other sleeve. "This one is harder to get off."

Laughter bellowed up from my gut. "Hard to get off, huh? Sounds about right."

"I got it!" She emerged from under my shirt, pulled the last sleeve off my arm, and dropped it to the floor. "Finally."

She walked to my front. "God, Zook. Look at you." She ran her fingers down the center of my chest, over my abs, and stopped at my belt buckle. We kissed hard as I walked her back to the bed, carefully helping her lay on her back.

"Your turn." I lifted her top over her head.

Oh holy fucking hell in a handbasket. What in the fucking heavens was she wearing? My eyes burned. A hideous... bra-like... thing covered her. Huge straps, lots of thick fabric. They were totally trapped in there.

"You look like a nun!" She wore that contraption for the entire plane trip? They must be suffocating.

"They didn't have anything else at the airport. This is what the women of Veranistaad wear under their clothes." She looked down at it and back up at me.

"Thank fucking god you aren't a woman of Veranistaad anymore. Take it off. Now! Not kidding. Get them out of there."

She giggled and reached behind her back to undo the fastenings.

As she unwrapped my precious gems, I pointed to the contraption. "And burn that thing."

Her wondrous breasts broke free, and I wanted to kiss them hello. Welcome back to the open air, darlings.

"Why're you so upset? It's only undergarments."

"Huh?" God, her breasts mesmerized me. Perfectly round globes, soft ivory skin, rosy pink nipples pebbling in the cool air.

She coughed and covered them with her arms. Darn. "Why did the bra bother you so much?"

Why? Isn't it obvious? "I don't know." I grabbed my hair and paced at the end of the bed. "It's upsetting seeing them like that. Reminds me of the Maidenform bras the women on the compound wore under their prairie dresses."

"Ahh. Disturbing. That's why you like the expensive lingerie so much."

I stopped at the foot of the bed and stared at her with my hands on my hips. "Let's not psychoanalyze my need to never see you wearing anything like that ever again. You need to be naked or wearing silk bras where your tits spill over the top. Or lace. Lace is acceptable. No more nun wraps."

"Okay." She laughed.

Absolutely not funny. She'd traumatized me. I glared at her to make her stop laughing, but she remained cruel, basking in my weakness.

"Come lie down." She patted the bedspread, keeping one arm over her breasts.

"Not feeling like lying down right now." Ugliest bra I'd ever seen. Shit.

She removed her arms from over her breasts and smiled.

Like a moth to a flame, I crawled up next to her and pulled her so our legs were side by side. My arm slid around her shoulders and twisted her until her tits pressed up against my bare chest. Bending one knee over my legs, she reached up and rubbed the stubble on my chin. "Better? Or you need to sulk over this a little longer."

"Better now. You're gorgeous whatever you wear. It's not you. It's the idea of you being bound. Didn't like the crown either. It was like a sign of ownership."

"Mmm. We're free of those bindings now."

"Yes." I bent my neck to kiss her sweet lips. Delicious. I didn't stop kissing her as I slid down and worked off her pants. I didn't dare glance at her underwear.

She climbed up and rode me backwards. I made sure her bandage wasn't rubbing on anything as I pulled her hair and teased her till she screamed for it. She came hard for me. Beautiful. Nothing in the world was better than the two of us together. I got lost in her as I came inside her. My girl. Back in my bed.

She collapsed on me and I wrapped both arms around her, pulling her back tight to my chest. Our breathing evened out, and I whispered in her ear. "Love you, CeCe. I'll never grow tired of watching you come apart and let go for me. Know what it means to you. Means a lot to me too."

"Yeah."

"You got that with me, always. Whatever you need to give me, you can. I'll be here. I'll gladly take it."

She turned in my arms, and her hair fell in my face. "Thank you."

"You need to talk about all the shit that went down with you, I'm here for that too. Lay it on me."

"Okay."

"But let me tell you one thing. What your parents did to you was not your fault. It says nothing about your value or worth. You are priceless to me."

She smiled her blissed-out grin. I tucked her into my side and pulled the covers up. We slept like that for hours. The sun passed the bedroom window and the sky turned a darker blue. When we woke, it was only four in the afternoon.

She wrapped her arm over my stomach and sighed.

I sang in her ear. "*Making love in the af-ter-noon with Cecelia.*"

She giggled. Glorious sound, her giggle.

"What's jubilation mean?" I asked her.

"Mmm." She hummed like jubilation was some yummy dessert. "Exultation, euphoria, extreme exuberance."

"Hmm?" My girl was so damn smart. Sexy big words coming out of her mouth like candy.

"Joy and happiness like you've never experienced."

"Ah, well then, the song fits the girl. You are jubilation."

She giggled again.

"What?"

"Nothing. Thank you. You're jubilation too."

I turned us so I was facing her as we both lay on our sides, my hand still under her neck gave her a squeeze.

"Did you sleep with anyone?" she asked me.

"No. Didn't want anyone else. I decided right after you left I'd find you. Worked my ass off to finish all the houses in the tract, so we could take off looking for you."

"You found me."

"Needle in a fucking haystack."

"How did you find me?"

"Rogan recognized your necklace." My fingers found the tiny clasp under her hair. "Let's take this thing off."

She grabbed it. "I can do it." Her hands attacked the clasp. She grunted and struggled with it.

"Turn around. Let me do it."

She paused and rolled over, lifting her hair for me to see the clasp.

"I wanna take this off you. You don't wear his brand anymore. When you're ready, you'll wear my ring. But it won't mean I own you. It means I love you."

She nodded and lifted her head to help me get the necklace out. I chucked it against the wall, and it fell to the floor. When I turned her back to facing me again, we both smiled. The noose around her neck was gone.

"You wanna teach?" I asked her after a while.

"I'd like to, yes."

"Where? Hale?"

She laughed. "Not Hale. Kids. Middle grade. High school. The time I missed in America."

"You got it."

"I need to earn my teacher's credentials."

"You will."

"I don't have any money. They don't pay you when you're a student teacher."

"Hey. Made it clear. You're living with me. I'll pay for whatever you need. You want another Mercedes, I'll get you one."

"I don't want a Mercedes."

"Whatever you want."

"I want a horse."

"You do?"

"I love horses. Always wanted one. Could you teach me how to ride?"

"Of course. This place has an empty stable and barn waiting. I'd love to do that for you."

"Is Orion still alive? She's your old horse from Idaho, right?"

"Yeah. Tessa brought her to Massachusetts. I asked Tessa about her. She said she's happy with Traveler and Rogan's dog on their ranch. We can go visit her anytime."

"That would be nice."

"By the way, we're going shopping tomorrow. New bras and underwear. Sexy. Matching."

"Kay."

Chapter 26

THE NEXT DAY, CECELIA and I lay side by side in the living room couch, her hand across my abs, her head on my chest and one leg draped over my knee. She'd slept for twelve hours, eaten breakfast, and now we were lying in front of a fire I'd made in the hearth. I watched her for signs of stress, but she seemed to be handling all that went down well. "Talked with Rogan while you were sleeping."

"What did he say?" She looked up at me with her endless macchiato eyes.

"He says he's in contact with Torrez. He'll make his move on Soraya within a week."

"Good. I'm nervous for her. Ivan and Yegor could take everything out on her, even though she had nothing to do with it."

"She's in good hands. He'll call us when he can." I gave her shoulder a squeeze and a rub. "Rogan's getting his FBI contacts involved. He thinks the Sharshinbaevs are trafficking women. Possibly men too."

"Really? I thought it was just me and Soraya."

I shook my head. "When he put his arm around your neck to subdue you, I knew then. It wasn't just the two of you. The look on his face. He handles lots of women like that. I don't know how many, but it's not just you and Soraya. You two were the floor models. They used you to attract buyers, promising them beautiful, educated women like you. They basically offered you to me for sale."

"God. That was so awful. I knew something was wrong, and I knew then I had to fight. I didn't care if he killed me."

"They told you you were a princess, but they forced you into it. I'll bet no one was getting paid. Fasul. All the workers who built the palace. All slave labor."

"I hope Rogan and the FBI put a stop to it. Can Rogan find a way to get Fasul out of there? And Nariam?"

"I asked him to look into it. If Rogan can't do it, Dallas runs a contractor for hire operation through Siege. We'll talk to him about Fasul and Nariam."

"Okay. So he's gone? We're free?" The hope in her eyes made me feel good. I gave her that freedom. She fought for it too. We did it together.

"Yes." I kissed the top of her head.

"Thank you for never giving up on me. You took a huge risk."

"Worst feeling in the world, knowing you were scared and alone over there. Didn't think of the risks at all. I'd do anything to get you back. Your life means more to me than my own."

She arched her neck and kissed me. "I love you. You're all that I am and everything I have." She used my own words on me.

"You and me together, Cecelia. We're meant to be. I'll fight like hell for you if anyone ever tries to get between us again."

She sighed and rested her cheek on my chest. Where it belonged.

"I have something I've been wanting to give you. Waited through graduation, the fire, six months without you. Not waiting a second longer."

Confusion, surprise, and love all passed through her face as she watched me drop to one knee and pull the box from my pocket.

"Want you to chase the wind with me. Forever."

"Oh my god!" She trembled and wrapped her arms around my neck.

I whispered in her ear the words I'd been holding in for far too long. "Be my wife. Be my everything."

She nodded into my neck. "I love you more than is sane for a woman to love a man. I never should've left you. I'll never leave you again."

We kissed and something inside me healed. My girl did that for me like I did for her. I opened the box and showed her the ring. Five carats total, a massive brilliant round diamond in the center, and two round side-stone diamonds. "If you want bigger or a different setting, I'll get it for you."

Her fingers trembled as she reached for it. "It's spectacular. No. I love it like this."

"Marry me out there on the rocks. At the edge of the sea." I slipped the ring on her left hand like I'd been dreaming of doing for a long time. "I'll see if I can get some migrators to fly over."

She laughed through the tears. "I don't need migrators."

"It'll be cool. Some geese, a few cranes. Maybe a pod of whales."

"Stop it."

"I'm serious. If you want pterodactyls to fly over, I'll arrange it."

"I don't need pterodactyls."

"Good, because I would never be able to spell that to order them."

Chapter 27

Cecelia

The day we picked for our wedding turned out to be unusually windy for June. The wedding planner suggested we move the ceremony inside, but I said no. I'd fight wind, rain, and anything else nature threw at me to marry Zook on our cliff.

My veil whipped behind me like the tail of a kite. The salty air stung my checks, blowing off all the makeup I'd carefully applied. I didn't care. As long as Zook was standing at the end of the aisle, I'd persevere.

I walked by myself. I didn't want anyone to give me away. I wanted to give myself to him. My breath hitched at the sight of Zook standing next to Destry. They wore matching black and white tuxedos with crimson silk ties and kerchiefs. They looked absolutely stunning and nearly identical. But I could tell my man apart. Mostly by his cowboy hat. But he also held a softness in his eyes. A fervent heat that glowed only for me. Destry's eyes had that feral cat nervousness, like he was itching to get out of his tux and out of his skin. Torrez stood next to Destry, also looking dashing in a tuxedo.

He'd made good on his promise to rescue Soraya and then proceeded to fall in love with her and marry her. She blossomed with her new freedom, becoming the independent woman she was meant to be with Torrez at her side the entire way. Soraya and I volunteered time and money to an organization to fight human trafficking and help victims recover from their ordeal. So many women had suffered much worse than we did, and we felt the least we could do was help them.

At the end of the short aisle, I stopped before Zook. My heart thudded and a swell of gratitude clogged my throat. We'd both fought long and hard for true love. And today we were celebrating it.

"You look exquisite." Zook lifted my veil, and his warm lips kissed my cheek.

The wedding dress Soraya and I picked out was fantastic. Not designer. We'd found it on the rack at a discount price, but the lace cutouts and mermaid tail fit my body like the dress was made for me. The maid-of-honor dress Soraya wore drew all the attention to her. A lacy Dolce & Gabbana slip dress with a low-cut square neckline and red satin straps. I didn't mind sharing the spotlight with my sister today. She looked fabulous and we were celebrating. She could wear whatever made her happy.

I handed Soraya my red and white bouquet of roses, and Zook took my hands. Despite the harsh wind, a peaceful calm passed through me. He smiled at me like he'd found his soul mate, and I returned the same smile because I knew I had.

The officiant's hair blew forward in the wind, and he held it down with his hand. "Zook, your vows."

Zook took off his hat and handed it to Destry. On cue, the wind stopped for a moment. Destry stilled, as did the small crowd in attendance at our little ceremony on a rocky cliff over the ocean.

Zook swallowed, and I watched his Adam's apple bob before he started to talk.

"I never knew jubilation."

Oh my gosh. I was going to cry.

"Couldn't spell it or comprehend it. Wouldn't even let anybody teach me."

I had to look away for a moment. His eyes. The love and intensity were too much. But only a second and then my eyes drew up to his again.

"Then you came into my life, and joy set root in my heart. It spread through my soul and erased all the dirt that had come before. My love for you will never die. It will grow evergreen. I'll never stop learning from you and loving you."

I sniffled, and his hands squeezed mine. A small smile quirked at the corner of his lips. "I promise to fill your life with jubilation and to love you unequivocally till I take my last breath."

His gorgeous smile grew wide and the wind picked up again, blowing my tears and veil back. He was smarter than any man at Hale.

"Cecelia?" The officiant nodded for me to say my part. Oh gosh. Could I do this?

"Zook, my love, my life." He smiled and nodded. "My wings were clipped for so long I'd given up hope. But you showed me the edge of the ocean. And I wanted to reach it. It seemed too far away, but you held out your hand. I only had to grasp it and let you guide me. I'm so glad I made the leap. In your arms, I'm safe to hide and free to soar. I promise to love you to the ends of the earth and sea forever."

He kissed me, and I didn't feel the wind or see the crowd. I only felt the complete wholeness of that kiss and the assurance I was the luckiest girl in the world.

WE MINGLED AT THE RECEPTION, which luckily was inside a clubhouse at the bottom of the bluff. I'd met Zook's mom and dad the day before. His mom loved the letter Zook wrote to him and left her old life behind. She had reconciled with Zook's dad, and they were living in Idaho. They looked so happy to have their family together again.

We visited with Rogan and Tessa first. Zook's friend, Gustavo, who had been released from prison, teased him about his upcoming concert tour.

"That's my twin brother. He's right over there." Zook pointed out Destry in the crowd. At the ceremony, Destry had sung a unique and moving version of "Make You Feel My Love."

"I know. Just teasing you," Gustavo replied.

Blythe, Locke, and some of Zook's crew mingled and seemed like they were having fun. Dallas brought his wife, Cyan, and I got to meet her. She was lovely and I thought we could be good friends.

After we finished a delectable dinner, Destry came up to us with a serious look on his face. "I'm going to find Lyric."

"Right now?" Zook asked him.

"Yes. It's time. If there's any chance at all we could have love like you have, I need to go for it. No more wasted time."

"Will you tell her everything?" I asked him.

"I'll tell her the truth. She needs to know. But most of all she needs to know how much I love her."

Zook patted him on the shoulder. "Good luck, brother. Go get her. You need anything, you call me."

"I will."

"You can stay with us anytime. Remember that when you feel lost. You always have a home here."

"Thank you."

Destry hugged us both and left the reception hall. Hopefully, Lyric would forgive him, and they could heal together.

The rest of the night went by in a blur. All I remembered was Zook smelling good, his warm hand ever present at the base of my spine or around my shoulder, the scratch of his tuxedo against the lace of my dress. Rogan and Tessa danced and gazed at each other, probably remembering their wedding. This was a night we'd look back on too and remember the day we pledged our love.

Epilogue

Zook

Five pelicans flew by in a line as I sat on my patio by my fire pit that I built and bought for myself.

Cecelia joined me with two plates of Boston cream pie, the special kind she makes with the cream cheese inside. She handed me a piece of pie, a fork, a beer, and a letter from ADX Florence in Colorado, the maximum security federal prison where Jeb would spend his dying days.

"This what it looks like?" I turned the letter over in my hands.

"If you mean a letter from Jeb Barebones, yes it could be. Open it."

My gut twisted for a second, but I brushed it off. I tore the top off the envelope and skimmed through the first half of his bullshit, but at the end something caught my eye.

I put the letter down and looked at my wife. "Jeb says he repents. He wants my forgiveness." Irony not lost in my tone.

She chuckled. "Does he now? Are you going to give it to him?" She took a bite of her pie, dragging her sexy lips over the fork to get every last bit of chocolate.

I took a bite too and savored the sweetness of the delicious food my wife made for me. "Nope. I'm not gonna give him that satisfaction, but I am gonna write a letter."

"To Jeb?"

"No, to Mr. Jensen."

"Who's Mr. Jensen?"

"He's our old neighbor from back on the compound in Caldwell. He's the one who needs this apology because he's the one who tried to help us and couldn't. He bought chickens from me, he gave Destry a guitar, he let Tessa read his encyclopedias. But there was nothing more he could do to help, and I'm sure it bugged him. I want to write him a letter and thank him for what he did for us. Shoot, I'm gonna send him the best damn chicken coop he's ever seen. Deluxe. Upstairs and downstairs, heating, lighting... a penthouse if his chickens want it. Maybe he needs a new barn."

She laughed.

I leaned back in my chair, interlocked my hands behind my neck, and looked up at the blue sky. "I hope Jeb wrote my mom a letter too because that would be therapeutic for her and Dad. Destry and Lyric might like an apology from Jeb, but she's on tour with him, and they probably don't give a shit."

She giggled. "Yeah."

"Right. I got all I want right here. The people who hurt you are either dead or under indictment. I'm helping you heal the holes they made in you. You're happy teaching. I got my own company, Gustavo working for me, a stable of horses, so no I don't need an apology from Jeb. Life could not be better than it is right now."

She finished her pie, and I tugged her hand to move her up on my lap. "My beautiful wife is making me a daddy. Never in a million years did I think I'd have a chance at something so wonderful as a child with a woman I loved so much. We'll give him all the things we never had. Stability. Integrity. Unconditional love. He'll learn to ride young. No bulls like Torrez' kid."

"It could be a girl." Damn, a mini Cecelia would have me wrapped around her finger. I'd love it.

"Doesn't matter. That child will be loved."

"Yes. If you love her like you love me, she'll be one very happy girl."

"But even without all that. If it were just you and me and nothing else, I'd still love you more than life. You're all that I am and all I'll ever have. Solely mine."

She ran her fingers through my hair and man it felt good. "You too, Zook. All I ever wanted but was too afraid to dream of having. It's frightening, you know. Having so much to lose. I could lose you, the baby..."

I kissed her forehead. "It is scary. But totally worth the risk. You're strong and you're brave. Together we're unstoppable. We won't lose it. We'll protect it till our dying day. Okay?"

She nodded. "Okay."

I picked my wife up and carried her to our bed. Then I showed her how unstoppable we were.

Want More Zook?

SIGN UP TO BEX DANE's VIP reader team and receive exclusive Men of Siege bonus content including;

- Deleted scenes from Zook

- Behind-the-scenes secrets no one else knows

- A sneak peek at the first chapter of Torrez

Give me more[1]!

---

1. https://www.subscribepage.com/bexzookdeletedscenes

Made in the USA
Middletown, DE
28 June 2019